Ten years is a long time to wait.

Michael Myers is a very patient man. And the wait is well worth it: he has a mission and nothing will stop him. He will search out and destroy the lone survivor of his last bloody rampage.

Doctor Loomis has watched Myers very closely for ten years. He knows first hand the evil festering beneath the calm exterior—his face bears hideous scars as a constant reminder. He knows Michael Myers is playing out a waiting game and he knows if Myers wins, the town of Haddonfield will lose.

It's Halloween and Michael Myers is going to treat the town to his bag full of tricks.

HALLOWEEN IV

A novel by
NICHOLAS GRABOWSKY

ISBN: 1-55547-292-3

Manufactured in the United States of America

Prologue

Haddonfield, Illinois, at one time long ago had been a peaceful town, just like any typical town away from the boisterous rumblings of factories and packed, bumper-to-bumper cars and buses and cabs on busy streets and intersections. Instead of smog, pollution, and haze, in Haddonfield there was only clear air, the sweet smell of homebaked apple pies cooling off on country porches and the joyous cries of children's laughter echoing forth from games of tag and jumprope beneath the shade of maple trees. This was a town of the seasons: a town where the magic of Christmas and the building of carrot-nosed snowmen waltzed with time's glorious dance of tradition; where Easter egg hunts and the July Fourth fire works show down at Fulbrook Park were anxiously awaited by everyone year after year.

And then there was Halloween.

Halloween used to be no exception to the thrilling festivities of yearly customs. Children never used to fear the night of October thirty-first, when they gathered their share of candy as they trick-or-treated down chilly sidewalks, usually getting treated and rarely getting tricked.

But the horror began back in nineteen sixty-three, when the scream of murder broke the Autumn silence in Haddonfield. And, years after, the horror returned, and this time to a more gruesome and terrifying magnitude.

Time had been unsuccessful in keeping away the horror; in the midst of innocence and quietude there is always a share of horror. It is a fact we all must face. But sometimes the horror goes away.

In Haddonfield, however, the horror keeps coming back.

Chapter One

A muddy wave rolled over the shoulder of the rain drenched road as the medical transport bus cut through the showers. The thick blackness of the night was illuminated only by the bus' headlights and an occasional flash of lightning. The crimson hues of Autumn burned from horizon to horizon but seemed to remain within the boundaries of the sky, disassociating themselves from the darkness of the world below. The sunset that separated day from evening was now but a memory on this, the thirtieth of October.

Somewhere within the far horizon, despite the encompassing darkness, a cold Fall breeze whispered through the fields of corn silent words of somber hush like a mother to her child, and the whisper found the industrial harvesters which in turn would soon rest in preparation for the following day's work. Crows remained perched on the shoulders of scarecrows until the wind grew from a whisper to a scream and the rain drove them off into the sky and the blackness.

In a clearing near the midst of the fields, paper witches riding brooms fell victims to the wet rain, and a cardboard skeleton which swung on a string like a hanged man from the same Birch tree met the same fate. At a farmhouse nearby, another row of skeletons looked on under the newly painted beams of the porch, almost in mock comparison to their comrades yards before them.

Back on the country road, rain washed the asphalt in sheets before the headlights of the transport bus. Within the bus, two Smith's Grove Medical personnel waited silently to reach their destination amidst emergency monitoring equipment and a space which would hold the gurney of the patient they awaited custody of. Heavy smoke filled the front section of the bus, smoke from the driver's filtered cigarette, and the nearly overweight security guard muttered something to nobody in particular before he let out a brief coughing fit which languished into a dreamless sleep. The driver suddenly felt it best for all concerned to turn on the radio, and found that as he did so nobody seemed to care either way. There were very few stations available to choose from, and he picked the one which emitted a familiar song, which he soon recognized as *Mister Sandman* by The Chordettes.

So what, he figured. *So I'm an oldies fan*.

And occasionally, between puffs, he mouthed a few of the words to himself. The ashes from the cigarette were tapped between each verse into a glass MURSEY HOTEL ashtray situated on the dashboard directly below a red and white sticker above the windshield which read THANK YOU FOR NOT SMOKING.

And the bus drove on.

It drove on through the pouring rain until the distant reaches of the headlight beams came across the gleam of the high security gates. The driver crushed his cigarette into the ashtray and flicked on his high beams which cut through the dark to disclose a sign on the right:

Ridgemont Federal Sanitarium

MAXIMUM SECURITY

Authorized Personnel Only

No Visitors

All Vehicles Subject to Search

High beams remaining on for the sake of a reasonably better view through the dimness, the driver made a right-hand turn into the driveway just past the sign and rolled the bus to a stop in front of the main gates. He waited as the gates slowly retracted, then proceeded to drive through as the guard beside him shifted in his seat and opened his eyes to the realization they had finally arrived. He swished away accumulated smoke from his face with his hand.

"Okay," the driver announced. "Time to party."

He switched off the radio, which was beginning to broadcast something which sounded like an old James Brown tune.

Inside the sanitarium, there was a security guard

seated in a large glass booth, a more bulky individual than the guard who remained within the bus outside. He gazed up at a fly buzzing around the lukewarm coffee in his I LOVE MY COCKER SPANIEL mug, the LOVE symbolized by a heart and the COCKER SPANIEL an undersized picture of a flop-eared mutt. He gave his crew cut a quick scratch before attempting to ward off the fly with his hand, grabbing at it rather than giving it a swat. He always tried to grab it perhaps out of boredom or perhaps because he actually hoped to catch the insect one day. Regardless, the circumstances were evident. But he didn't exactly hate his job, however boring it seemed. As a matter of fact, he favored his surroundings more than any other aspect of his work experience. It was most likely due to his father being an architect and his desire to follow in his footsteps, but he was deeply interested in how Ridgemont was actually a penitentiary which had been built in the late 1920's. Fifty-year-old light fixtures hung above slowly rotating ceiling fans. Beams of painted wood stretched from wall to wall. Of course, it was no work of art. But the guard didn't exactly like ART. He liked OLD. He liked NOSTALGIA.

Anyway, nothing could truly say much for his job now that he thought about it; he was still known to all of his Friday night buddies at Larry's Bar as the GUY WHO WORKS IN A LOONEY BIN.

What the hell. Somebody has to guard this place. Make sure no crazy gets out. Sometimes crazies

10

get in, and they don't even hafta be the damn patients, either.

He tested the coffee with his finger to make sure it really *was* lukewarm, then swirled around what little cream there was floating towards the center. He thought he heard what sounded like snoring. He turned and saw his companion guard on the stool beside him as always, but he was simply clearing his throat and turning another page of FIELD AND STREAM. Turning back to his coffee, the fly gone to return again possibly later, the guard looked up and saw the two attendants from Smith's Grove. He withdrew his finger from the coffee and set the mug down next to a small stack of paper work. He gave his crew cut another quick scratch.

"Good evening," one of the attendants spoke cheerlessly. The other attendant, a woman, looked on with much the same enthusiasm. "We're from Smith's Grove . . ."

No shit, the guard thought, seeing that it was written several times over their uniforms.

"All metal objects into the tray on your left," he told them.

There weren't very many objects for this tray, and the guard barely managed them a glance. He was busily sorting out the paper work before him, found something on a clipboard, and proceeded to jot something down. He continued talking.

"Purpose of visit?"

"Patient pickup and transfer to Smith's Grove," the male attendant answered.

11

Another clipboard. More jotting. Another sip of coffee.

"All right," he said. "Hold on a second. I'll take you down there myself."

The guard grabbed the last clipboard and stood up from his seat. His fingers disappeared under the counter and a buzzing issued forth the news that the two could now enter the glass door through the side. He joined them as the other guard with the magazine took his place at the window, reaching for the SPANIEL coffee mug. The guard with the attendants turned to him.

"I got mono," he warned, half jokingly.

The guard set the coffee mug down.

The two attendants followed the guard down a silent corridor.

"You're late," he told the two. He wasn't angry; he was simply inviting conversation.

"Yeah, well, you should be on the road," the male attendant exclaimed.

"Helluva night, huh?" the guard said.

"Real charmer."

The guard led the two attendants down the empty corridors, silent save for the echoes of their footsteps against the grey stone floors. They passed a series of small see-through offices, a janitor's supply closet, and employee restrooms and they arrived at what the guard referred to confidentially as the "corridor of the crazies." The three of them beheld locked ward doors with small square windows. There were faces behind the windows; faces of human beings. The degenerates of society. Some appeared to be distressed and physically damaged, but what they all had in common—the attendants swiftly noticed—was each one of them displayed the same emotion: some sort of agony. For some, the agony distorted their physical appearance, creating elongated arms and cheekbones as if from starvation. Others were beyond pain, simply staring blankly into empty space. Staring. Forever staring.

"First time here?" the guard asked the two behind him.

"Hope it's the last time," the woman remarked.

"You never get used to them," the guard said, keeping his eyes ahead of him, not looking up. "You never get used to the faces."

As they passed, the three felt the eyes of the onlookers gazing out, watching them, gawking at them. Their faces pressed to the glass, molding their features into the undersized panes, one man's scar tissue rubbing off and leaving a crimson smear, his hot breath a steamy film.

The woman turned away, disgusted. "They're *all* criminally insane?"

"They're here, aren't they?" the guard replied. He scratched his head once more. The woman noticed a layer of dandruff dots dusting the shoulders of his uniform. "Over there," he pointed, "we got a man use to pick up hitchhikers, you see, take their picture, bath 'em, cut 'em up, bake 'em in a stewpot. Left side we got a woman does everything in threes. Buried three husbands, three children, alive you know. Next to her is an obstetrician. He murdered every ninth child he delivered, then stole their bodies and kept them in this huge nursery in his basement. We even have a ten-year-old who had his family for Christmas dinner. Literally. Took the leftovers to school and handed them out as sandwiches to his friends.''

A saneless wail issued out from one of the rooms as they passed, and the woman exhaled a languished vociferation of intermingled dismay and disgust as she caught sight of a small boy's face against another window, his eyes widened to the extent they appeared to be lidless.

The male attendant uttered a slight groan. "Jesus Christ."

"Christ got nothing to do with this place," the guard muttered.

Up ahead, the gaping mouth of an elevator awaited their admission. They obliged the invitation and entered. The doors joined, and the guard turned to them. He was neither smiling nor frowning; but his gaze was that of pure dread.

It was times like these he hated his job. He'd much rather be swirling his finger in lukewarm coffee back at the front desk, combating flies. Now, he was forced to combat fear.

"This," he said, "is where society dumps its worst nightmares." The harsh grinding of their mechanical descent was frighteningly boisterous, and the woman attendant thought it wise to simply keep her eyes glued to the level indicator and her mind not on the human abominations viewing them in the corridors but rather harnessing it within her skull. As sub-levels ticked off one by one, the security guard had to raise his voice over the reverberating noise to continue. "Just talking about the one you're picking up gives me the willies. Decade ago, Halloween night, killed sixteen people. Maybe more. Out to get his sister. Nearly got her, too, the poor woman. But his doctor, of all people, his *doctor* shot him six times, and the bugger got away. The doc found him again, shot him, set him on fire—both of 'em nearly burned to death. Glad to see this one gone. Yes indeed."

The indicator was at the lowest level. The elevator jolted to a stop. The woman attendant drew her breath in. The guard looked at her.

"Welcome to hell."

He raised his hand to a wall mounted lockdown latch, and the elevator doors opened to yet another pair of doors, steel-caged, which in turn came open with an agonizing creak thus sounding forth their arrival.

Truly this is hell, thought the woman as she was first introduced to the rush of forced air heating which greeted her out of the shadows. *Of course, this isn't the hell I imagined growing up in Sunday school, with the ol' fire and brimstone, but it's just as bad. Maybe worse. This place is silent; warm, but somewhere within the warmness there's an underlying coldness. And it's dark. So damn dark.*

Ward "E" was just like that, with a few extra added attractions. There were two people the guests could see thus far, one appeared to be an orderly swamping the floor with soapy water next to a

15

steel bucket, nodding rythmically to the music blaring from his headset which was attached to a small radio hanging from his front pocket. *Probably the only measure of life around*, both attendants figured coincidentally. At least by measure of life as they knew it.

The other figure was that of a young woman who stood below a single, naked yellow light bulb which dangled, the chain falling into her face unnoticed. She stood beside a windowless steel door opened to distinct dimness and, together with the bulb overhead, it gave her a sort of sinister countenance. As the three proceeded forward in her direction, the darkness revealed vacant spring framed single beds, old with rust, near silent medical equipment. The Ridgemont nurse moved from her stance under the light and spoke into the room beside her.

"The transfer personnel are here, Doctor," she said.

Suddenly the dimness of the light issuing from within the room was interrupted, and the shadow of another figure appeared. The doctor stepped into the light. He seemed calm, although there was a certain vague expression of relief in his eyes, an expression only a keen observer could readily detect. He had journeyed through the trials of growing old and was continuing to do so with undeniable anguish at the present age of forty-five. His hair was cut short, a mixture of brown and grey, and the above light seemed to swirl the colors, making them come alive; it played luminary games with

16

the profound wrinkles embedded in his forehead and cheeks.

"Smith's Grove?" he questioned the attendants. His voice was commanding, yet somehow either age or occupation gave him a certain somber resonance.

The male attendant nodded. "Yes."

The doctor offered a hand to the male. "I'm Doctor Hoffman, medical administrator."

"Has he been prepped?" the attendant asked.

The doctor answered, "Ready to go. All I have to do is sign him out, then he's all yours."

As the two attendants began to follow Doctor Hoffman, who turned and headed back into the cell, the nurse motioned the security guard to follow her in the opposite direction. The guard gratefully obeyed.

The first objects the two attendants saw in the room was the gurney and the figure which the gurney held. The figure was motionless and darkened by the absence of light in its corner of the room. They could partially see the outline of its face, and a closer inspection revealed there were heavy bandages covering its entirety. The rest of the body was garbed in nothing but a grey gown and was in turn covered halfway with a white sheet. An IV needle and apparatus protruded from each arm like tiny, unmoving serpents.

This was their man.

This was their patient.

The second bed in the room was flanked by silent monitoring equipment stationed in a corner, diagonal to that of their patient. This bed was unmade, and the imprint showed there had once been a body in that space. Probably moved out like theirs would be. Probably dead.

The woman attendant stepped closer to the patient. "You say he's been in a coma for ten years?"

"That's right," the doctor answered, his amazement worn thin. However, the presence of company somewhat revived his astonishment. "With bullet wounds and severe burns. It's incredible that he's still alive."

"A lot of people wish he weren't," the male attendant remarked, remembering the stories he had heard, the stories passed down from employee to employee at Smith's Grove.

The doctor stepped over to the wall adjacent to the rear of the steel door and grabbed a clipboard stationed on a rack. As he withdrew a pen from one of the pockets in his white smock, the woman moved over to the body. In the meantime, the male handed papers he took from a shirt pocket and exchanged them with another paper from the doctor. Each man initialed his set of papers and the doctor slipped his set onto the clipboard and made another notation. The woman gazed at the body, lingering for a moment, almost afraid to touch it, then proceeded to check one IV needle followed by the other. Behind her, the two others were moving back out into the ward.

The male attendant spoke to the doctor as he waited for the signing of documents. "I'd assumed

Doctor Loomis would be here. Michael Myers is still his patient.''

Indignant, the doctor looked up and gazed into the eyes of the man. He had ceased scribbling. "This is a legal mandate. Any patient stable for a continuous ten year period must be remanded to State psychiatric authority. This isn't medical, therefore, this matter doesn't concern Doctor Loomis.''

"I was simply saying it's usual procedure to inform the case doctor.''

The doctor returned the remainder of the signed documents. "If Loomis read memos, he'd be standing here right now. Fortunately, his position is more ceremonial than medical. And with Myers gone from here, my hope is the good doctor will either transfer, retire, or die.''

Inside the cell, the woman continued tending to the shape in the corner. Pulse. Pressure. Breathing was slow and steady.

This was the man—the *thing* that had murdered all those people. She'd heard about it; heard the stories. But they were all just that—*stories*. The same as reading a newspaper or a magazine. And here lay the story incarnate, right before her eyes. She gazed down upon it, upon those bandages. *Pure evil*, someone had told her before she departed from Smith's Grove. *Pure evil behind those bandages, those scars behind those bandages*.

She forced her eyes away. Satisfied with the patient's condition, she called out behind her, "All right, let's move him out.''

As she turned away, a naked hand slipped out

from beneath the gurney sheet. The attendant, startled upon hearing the rustling, quickly spun around. Her hand went tremulously to her chest as if to ensure the restraint of her heart.

The hand had simply fallen off the gurney. She had been checking the patient, checking the IV needles, and the hand had eventually slipped because it had been disturbed.

That was all.

That was it.

(Actually, it was more like *she* had been disturbed.)

The hand was hanging there, limp, deformed by tight shiny pink burn scars, webbed with ropy keloids of knotted flesh, and it was *doing nothing else*.

So, having placed herself back into the comforting analgesic of her senses, she was ready to move the patient.

****

Outside, the attendants rolled the gurney with the comatose body up the pavement to the rear of the opened bus as the driver and the hefty security guard who hated smoke watched. The attendants snapped up the wheels and locked them, lifting the gurney and shoving it into the back until it disappeared. After doing so, the male unexpectedly backed into Doctor Hoffman, who had escorted them outside.

The woman, her mind growing all the more

curious about this dark human monstrosity, asked the doctor if there were any living relatives.

"A niece living in his hometown," replied the doctor. "Too young to act as legal ward."

After they strapped the gurney in place, the woman announced it was locked and loaded, and they were ready to rock and roll.

" 'Night, Doc," the male said.

The doctor looked them over one final time as the team prepared to leave.

"Drive carefully," he told them.

The transport bus drove away, disappearing down the rain washed country road and into the night.

Chapter Two

Sunday was a medium-sized black labrador that enjoyed spending time during the early hours of the morning up and about, scrounging around throughout the house for anything interesting or edible overlooked by the human beings before they had gone to sleep hours before. He loved the quiet almost as much as the times when the family would be up and about and playing with him and Rubber Porcupine, only in a different way. At night, when they were asleep, he enjoyed the fact there were no watchful eyes to see what little mishap he could get into. But tonight something was a trifle different, although not unlike the past few mornings. Someone was up and about, and the black labrador sensed it. There was a stirring somewhere downstairs, probably in the livingroom. Sunday had been sitting next to a large window at the end of the hall upstairs, watching the rain, watching the lightning strike in the horizon, illuminating the area where it sat. He padded across the carpet, past the master bedroom where the heads of the household soundly slept. Down the staircase he went and into the livingroom to where the movement was on the lap of the couch.

It was the little girl.

He liked the little girl very much, ever since she suddenly became a part of the family not long ago; a welcomed new face. Sunday didn't mean to startle her as he jumped and landed at her side. He had found a hand to lick and one that would pet him in turn.

The six-year-old girl had been sitting there for some time, surrounded by a brigade of pillows, occasionally gazing out the window into the dark, rain filled street; gazing at the lightning, unafraid, much as Sunday had done. Her thoughts were not languishing tiredly as could have been supposed; her thoughts were numerous and upon many things. Thoughts of her past. Thoughts of her present. Tired, weary, melancholy thoughts of a time gone by and a time she could never again bring back. Only memories, faded and distant—memories that made lonely little girls cry.

"Hey, kiddo." A familiar voice. "It's four in the morning."

She turned away from the window to gaze upon Rachel. She knew Rachel wanted to help, but her presence only brought another flood of remembrances to mind. Rachel always tried to pretend she was her big sister, but little Jamie knew perfectly well she wasn't. In fact, she didn't even

24

have a *real* family like Rachel did at all. Rachel had told her once that she herself was a lonely six-year-old at one time, and that even now she was a lonely seventeen-year-old. But Rachel didn't know what loneliness was, really, did she?

All Jamie could tell her was that she couldn't sleep.

There went Rachel's eyes, getting all big again, like she was going to say something smart and loving.

"What is this, four nights in a row? You going for a record here? Six-year-old insomniac's hall of fame?"

Then the words just came out. She wasn't sure whether she *wanted* the words to come out, but there they were. "Do you love me, Rachel?"

"Oh, serious questions tonight," she said quietly, trying to be a bit humorous at reassuring her. She too was petting the dog. "Of course I love you."

"Like a sister?"

"Jamie."

"Like a *real* sister?"

Rachel sighed. She paused for a moment to think, attempting to search for the right words. If only she could get Jamie to understand. If only they both could get some sleep. "You know we're not really sisters, Jamie. You know we can't help that. But that doesn't mean that just because we're not *real* sisters I love you any less."

Jamie's gaze returned to the window; back to the rain.

"Sure it does," she muttered.

She didn't notice it at first, and when she did, she paid it no mind; there was a new object in the street across the way, through the rain and the haze. All she knew was that it looked like a large van. She could not see the insignia of Smith's Grove imprinted on the side, but she noticed briefly that the rear doors were opened and the vehicle itself was void of movement and silent.

She was distracted. Rachel was turning her around to face her.

"Jamie," she told her, "I know you miss your parents. It hasn't been that long . . ."

"It's been eleven months," she cut her off.

Another sigh from Rachel. The dog rested its head on the little girl's lap. "Your mom used to baby-sit me when I was your age. I bet you didn't know that."

"You're lucky," Jamie said. "I wish she could do the same for me."

Rachel took the little girl into her arms and embraced her in a moment of silent thought, lovingly. "Come on, kiddo. Back to bed."

By the hand, Rachel led a weary Jamie up the stairway and to the threshold of Jamie's bedroom, followed by a contented Sunday. She knelt down and gave the little girl a soft kiss on the cheek.

"Sleep tight, sweetie," Rachel said. "French toast for breakfast. Night-night."

And with a slight pat on the head, she closed Jamie's bedroom door and left her once again to her thoughts.

The same old room surrounded her, every detail a symbol of her new family's attempts to make her their own, to make her feel like one of them nestled under their wings. Various doll faces stared back at her from shelves against the wall and from the top of her pink dresser. An assemblage of toy rhinos and penguins and bears and horses congregated around her light blue and red toy box near her bed. Across from them were plush vegetables and fruits with inquisitive expressions as if having formed their own clique at the foot of the bed. There were Sesame Street wall hangings, the characters being of the same sort embroidered onto her pajamas and pompom slippers. There were clowns in the rocking chair near her closet.

She felt a tremendously cold chill which drew her attention to the bedroom window. It was open, and the wind and drizzle were blowing into the curtains and onto the carpet, dampening them. Jamie scurried across the room and drew the window shut.

Lightning flashed once as she turned toward the bed; if her gaze had been directed toward the window, she would have seen the reflection of the figure that had entered her room, a tall figure behind her illuminated for but a moment's time after which returning into the darkened shadows.

She was not alone.

Moving past her dresser, Jamie opened the double doors to her closet. There was a tan shoe box before her on the floor near an assortment of tennis shoes. She reached for it and removed the top.

More memories. This time, the memories were materialized in photographs—pictures of times gone by: a photo of her mother, Laurie Strode. On the back, in faded pencil, were the words MOM AT SEVENTEEN. There was a birthday card from four years ago—WITH LOVE FOR OUR LITTLE GIRL. There was a picture of Jamie, two years ago, riding her father piggyback at the Great American amusement park. Here was another picture, all of them together having a barbeque with the Hammets, their neighbors, her father posing as the Master Chef of the Grill, reddened chicken breasts flaming beside him over coals. Memories—nothing but memories.

One more flash of lightning. Above her, to her left, unnoticed, was the figure, the shape—within the confines of her closet. The brilliant flash revealed its face, rows of whitened streaks surrounding two hollow cavities where the eyes should be, as if it were encased within bandages.

Again, Jamie did not see the figure; at the moment when she very well could have, there was now—

darkness.

Jamie returned the shoe box to the litter of tennis shoes on the floor, then turned and went for her bed. Kneeling, she pulled the covers down further to slip inside and before she did, she clasped her hands somberly and prayed a simple prayer, a slight rendition of what her true parents had once taught her.

"Now I lay me down to sleep, I pray the Lord

my soul to keep. If I should die before I wake, I pray the Lord my soul to take. God bless Mr. and Mrs. Caruthers. God bless Rachel, God bless Sunday, God bless me, and God bless Mommy and Daddy in heaven. Amen.''

With that, she began to rise to slip under the covers.

Suddenly she was distracted. There was a shuffling sound—something stirring. It stopped just as suddenly as it had begun. She realized it came from the closet. She turned and gazed into its emptiness.

Silence.

She continued her gaze.

Nothing.

Jamie rose to her feet and stepped toward the opened closet door. Hesitantly, she peered closer into the black obscurity of clothes and boxes.

A fallen rag doll.

She returned it to the top of one of the boxes. Satisfied and somewhat relieved, she turned once again to the bed. But she closed the closet doors, just to ease her mind.

Yet another sound.

Again she turned, and this time she beheld the inner emptiness of the closet as the door opened just a crack, then yawning wider as if in an ambiguous introduction to an entity about to make a grand appearance. She remembered Mr. Caruthers reading to her a few days ago from the funny papers—something about a closet of anxieties.

But there was still nothing.

A different sound. Branches against the window glass; the maple tree outside. *Scratch . . . scratch.*

She gazed back at the hollow abyss before her. It beckoned her, called for her, teased her. Sighing, she stepped up to it to close it once more.

That was when she heard the breathing.

All of a sudden something grabbed her—grabbed her ankle; she felt the muscular grip tighten and pull.

It came from beneath the bed.

She screamed.

She stumbled as the monstrous hand pulled her down, causing her to topple onto the hard carpet, landing on her arm. She shrieked in pain. She kicked and writhed frantically, but her efforts were useless seeming only to heighten her assailant's efforts. Her mind was racing in a merry-go-round of circles amidst the panic. She was being pulled under . . . under . . .

. . . under . . . a second hand came forth . . . reaching . . .

and suddenly she managed to break free. With no further thought, she scrambled to her feet awkwardly, her shrieks echoing forth into all directions around her. She didn't notice the shape of the man rising from the far side of the bed, or the butcher knife which gleamed with the strike of lightning. She went for the door. Her hand reached for the knob, her fingers gripped it firmly, and she pulled the door open.

There he was, before her. It was no use. In the midst of her screams, death was raised in the form of a knife. As it struck, her last thoughts within the haze told her she would soon meet Mommy and Daddy.

****

. . . and then the closet door opened. The bedroom light streamed onto her face as she opened her eyes and stared into the desperate faces of Mr. and Mrs. Caruthers. Still, Jamie held tight to the shoe box huddled with her in the corner surrounded by hanging dresses and colored cardboard boxes and dolls. Mrs. Caruthers pushed some of the dolls aside and held the little girl close. She noticed Rachel not far behind, gripping Sunday by his collar.

"Dear God," Darlene Caruthers exclaimed, hushing the little girl's cries, consoling her. "It's all right, sweetheart. A bad dream, that's all. Just a nasty old dream. I've got you. You're safe. See? Just let it go, honey. Put it out of your mind."

As Jamie reached out to embrace her in turn, the shoe box fell, toppling over the tennis shoes, its contents spilling. A black and white photograph, yellowed with age, rested face up. Between the near-white boundaries, a six-year-old boy in a bright clown costume was standing beside his older sister. In the background was a house, jack-o-lanterns aglow on the front porch, orange sky accenting the scenery over the far horizon.

It was Michael and Judith Myers.

It was Halloween, 1963.

Chapter Three

The booming of footsteps echoed down the dreary corridors of the Ridgemont Federal Sanitarium. It was Halloween morning, and the sunshine of the new day streamed through the high windows of the first floor hallways and down upon the inner offices. Shadowing the offices, obscuring the sunlight, was the stout silhouette of a man hurrying to pass. His cane accompanied the echoes of every determined, acrimonious footfall. Staffers garbed in white stepped out of the figure's path, their gazes following, and they were soon joined by others who watched from doorways, faces filled with both curiosity and a grudging respect.

The figure stepped up to the last office in the corridor, the one on the right. On the window of the door the letters read ADMINISTRATOR'S OFFICE. He wasted no time throwing this door open, slamming it against a row of metal file cabinets inside. Doctor Hoffman, startled, gazed up from the payroll reports on his desk and into the virulent eyes of Doctor Loomis.

To Doctor Hoffman, Doctor Loomis was the sort of person who took his work too seriously; seriously to the extent of becoming obsessed with any patient that managed to trigger off some deep, morbid interest Loomis held within himself. To Hoffman, everyone involved would be better off with this whole Michael Myers business if he had simply perished in the flames ten years ago, even better with Mr. Myers. The only evidence of the fire was the deep, burn scar that looked like a course of runnels trailing down the right side of Loomis' face. Some minor attempts at plastic surgery had not managed much visible repair of the disfigurement. And for some reason, the man seemed to age twice as fast as a normal human being. He was a determined man, two-fisted in dialogue and imposing in appearance, however old he sometimes appeared.

He marched up to Hoffman's desk and leaned over angrily. His voice was harsh. *"Why wasn't I notified?"*

Hoffman stood his ground. "About what?"

"You know damn well about what! You let them take It out of here."

"Doctor Loomis. Michael Myers was a federal patient, and a federal prisoner. Therefore, he was subject to federal law."

Loomis was furious. "We're not talking about just another federal prisoner, Hoffman. We're talking about Evil on two legs!"

34

"For chrissake," Hoffman complained, "spare me the speech. I've listened to it for a decade. The fact is your evil monster has been in a nonreversible coma for ten years and in that coma he will stay until his heart and brain say stop."

Loomis stepped backwards. "He's been waiting . . ."

"I've said it before . . . I think *you're* the one who needs mental help. You're *obsessed* with this thing. The staff tells me you stand for hours just looking at him." He sat up within his chair, leaning forward, as if he were about to rise. "Tell me objectively, Loomis. Is this normal professional medical behavior?"

"Do you know what today is?" The doctor with the cane shouted. "Do you know the date? Every day I look in the mirror. Every day I remember. I tell you . . . I don't want anyone to have to live through that night again."

Hoffman let out a fatigued sigh. "I can see this is useless."

"Where was he taken?" Loomis demanded.

"Smith's Grove. He's probably there by now."

"Call!"

"What?"

Loomis drew closer to the desk. "Call Smith's Grove. Set my mind at ease. Fuel your sarcasm. I hope to God I'm wrong about what I feel. *Call!*"

Why is this man wasting my time? Hoffman thought wearily. *Why the hell doesn't this man just take that goddamn cane of his and his goddamn Michael Myers horror stories and just leave me alone?*

35

Oh, what the hell.

Hoffman picked up the phone to his right and dialed. At last there was silence in the room. If he could only get this over with . . .

"Yes," he spoke into the receiver, "this is Doctor Hoffman at Ridgemont. We had a patient transferred there just last night, Michael Myers. That's right."

Loomis waited, impatient. Suddenly, Hoffman's face was overcome by a touch of dejection.

"I see," Hoffman continued. "All right, thank you." He hung up the phone. The room remained silent for a moment, Loomis awaiting the inevitable. Hoffman continued his gaze upon the desk, not looking up, but not ashamed that he had been wrong. On the contrary; it was still *Loomis* that was crazy. It was still Loomis that was *wrong*. Of course everything was all right. But tell a man like Doctor Loomis that and see if he agrees with you. "They're two hours overdue. But they don't feel that it's a cause for concern . . ."

When he looked up, he found he was conversing with empty air. The doctor was gone, the door still swung wide against the file cabinets.

Dammit!

"Loomis," he called out, and was answered only by the repercussions of his own voice throughout his head. *"Loomis!"*

****

Doctor Loomis marched across the puddled pavement in the direction of a half-dozen blue OFFI-

CIAL USE federal sedans, his hard black shoes splashing droplets of water onto the legs of his dark brown slacks. He stormed over to the nearest vehicle and opened the door to the driver's side with a key from his pocket key chain. He heard a distant voice behind him; perhaps it was the voice of reason, but regardless, Loomis was not a reasonable man in the face of unreasonable urgency. But he recognized that voice, and this was the very reason why he did not turn.

"Where do you think you're going?" Hoffman said, catching his breath. He had been running.

Loomis continued into the car, slammed the door shut and rolled down the window. His words were hurried and desperate. "To find It. It has a single relative left alive—the daughter of Laurie Strode. She'll be Its target now."

Hoffman gripped the edges of the car door with despairing urgency. "For godsake, just listen to yourself. Michael Myers is a threat to no one."

"Even after ten years," Loomis replied, starting the engine, "you still have no idea what you've let loose." Then, "What are you doing?"

Hoffman had hastened over to the passenger's side, opened the door and hopped in.

"If you're wrong," he said, "I don't want you starting a panic."

"And if I'm right?"

"You won't be," Hoffman told him.

But there was that encompassing fear.

****

37

Four Illinois State Highway Patrol cars were parked on the shoulder of the dust-filled country highway. A state trooper was in the process of lighting flares, placing them across the asphalt of the breakdown lane, occasionally raising his gaze to the remote distance of the road and wiping the sweat from his brow. The area was silent save for the crackling of the patrolmen's radios and the talking. Three troopers were working their way down a muddy embankment beyond the shoulder which sloped down into a deep ravine of marshy undergrowth.

The Smith's Grove medical transport bus rested on its roof; a wasted dissolution at the bottom of the ravine. Ground fog swirled and eddied around shattered bits of glass and metal.

The three troopers scattered around the wreckage, investigating the surroundings carefully.

"What a mess," the first one exclaimed. Then, to the others, "Swing around the backside. Anyone alive is a lucky son of a bitch."

"Anyone alive'd be too messed up to be a lucky son of a bitch," another remarked.

The troopers circled the vehicle, slowly moving nearer through sucking mud and swamp runoff. The youngest of the three sloshed towards the rear quarter, finding the back doors twisted open. He peered into darkness. The other two joined him there, gazing closer into the bus' interior. As soon as they began to realize what they beheld, repulsion set in and the younger one dodged over to a nearby clump of weeds, doubling up, retching into the thickness. Another newly arrived trooper, a much older man, nearly stumbled over to the other two and joined them as they continued their gaze inside.

"Holy shit," he whispered. "Looks like those traffic films we show to Driver's Ed classes."

A trooper beside him unbuckled a flashlight from his belt and flashed it within the bus for a better view. Behind him, still others circled through the weeds.

Back out on the highway, Loomis' sedan joined the patrol cars pulled over to the shoulder. He killed the engine and stepped out, gravel crunching under his heels. Hoffman shut the door on the other side. Hoffman walked over to the embankment and in dismay followed Loomis' gaze down the slope to the overturned vehicle. Doctor Loomis appeared calm, sounded calm, but Hoffman noted there was a seriousness, a cast of despair within his eyes; always that despair.

"Is that it?" Loomis asked Hoffman.

"Yes," he answered regretfully. A state trooper approached them, and Hoffman turned to him. It was time to be serious, terribly serious, as was his fellow professional with the cane. But there was no need for panic. The circumstances were very simple: Michael Myers was *dead*. If not, he was laying seriously injured down there in the wreckage. He must believe that; to do otherwise would place himself at the same level as the overly negative, paranoid doctor beside him. Emotions aside, he asked the trooper, "Do you know when this happened?"

"Sometime during the night. They probably lost the road in the storm. Went off the embankment. It happens."

Hoffman turned back to Loomis. Perhaps the good doctor would *now* realize what *really* happened here. "An accident," he said plainly.

Loomis started up, "Do you really think that . . ."

"Why shouldn't I?" Hoffman told him.

"How many staff on the bus?" Loomis snapped.

"Four plus Myers."

Loomis turned to the trooper immediately. The baldness of his forehead was streaming with sweat. "How many bodies have you found?"

"Hard to tell," the trooper answered. "They're all pretty chewed up."

Determined, Loomis started down the embankment. The Ridgemont administrator called after him. "Loomis. It's over. Leave it alone!"

He threw his hands into the air in total frustration. The trooper beside him shook his head and gave a half amused sort of grin.

"Oh, hell." Hoffman went off down the embankment in turn.

Loomis carefully approached the wreckage, not minding the filth and mud encasing his shoes as much as what he feared he would find, or, rather, what he would *not* find, up ahead. He scrutinized each piece of metal; studied every bit and portion of the accident as he passed. Finally, he reached the twisted metal doors and poked his head heedfully inside.

Coming up on the rear, Hoffman in turn made

40

his way to the twisted doors of the bus. He met Loomis' dismal frown.

"He's not here," Loomis proclaimed. "He's gone. Dammit, he's *gone*."

Hoffman felt a sudden sense of anguish; a sense of profound uneasiness. It was like waking up to what you thought was a nightmare only to soak up the realization that the terror was truly taking place. He called out to a trooper nearby. "Have you found any other bodies?"

"Not yet," was the response. "There's a lot of ground to cover."

"You won't find him," Loomis insisted. "He did this. Now he's escaped."

"You don't know that," Hoffman said. "Michael could have been thrown from the bus."

The trooper agreed, "I've seen bodies thrown fifty, sixty feet from a crash site."

Hoffman continued, "And even if by some miracle Michael *is* conscious, his muscles will be useless. The man's been ten years flat on his back. Immobile. Give the troopers time to search."

Loomis wasn't listening. He was preoccupied with something else, something on the ground, something nobody else seemed to notice. He needed a closer look to be sure, and, with the tip of his cane, he raised the metal object for a better inspection. The object was an earring, gold, or at least gold plated, a small glimmering star hanging from the ring itself. Attached to the earring was something pale. A piece of flesh.

A human ear lobe.

Loomis turned back to the other two. "You're talking about him as if he were a human being. That part of him died years ago."

He dropped the object and immediately proceeded up the embankment, Hoffman calling after him.

"*Now* where are you going?"

"To Haddonfield," he yelled in return. "It's a four hour drive. You can reach me there through the local police. Four hours should be long enough for you to find him if he's here. If you don't, then I am sure I will . . ."

Hoffman and the other trooper gazed on as the doctor strode up the muddy embankment using his cane as a lever. For one moment, it appeared as if he were about to fall. He reminded Hoffman of some sort of minikin nobleman, waving his cane about in an effort to gain footing up the slope. He gave a disconcerted sigh as Loomis disappeared over the shoulder and onto the highway.

Even with all the pandemonium of the searchers, Loomis' sedan engine could still be heard.

"What's his story?" the trooper asked Hoffman.

"You don't want to know."

Chapter Four

It was another peaceful Autumn morning in the tranquil community of Haddonfield, Illinois. Birds sang gleefully within the auburn branches of maple trees and the cool morning breeze scattered leaves playfully over grass dampened by the previous night's showers. An occasional car cruised leisurely down the quiet street, every so often catching a puddle and splashing it over the curb. In the distance, a lone paperboy was making his rounds, hurling morning editions with long practiced ease from a sturdy blue bicycle.

The very first sounds in the kitchen echoed throughout the Caruther household, and soon afterwards were followed by the usual, daily hustle-and-bustle of hurried family members moving to and fro, munching down some sort of breakfast so they could hurry to work or to school; the kind of confusion which had become so commonplace that no one had time to give any thought to how confusing things were.

Richard Caruthers had just finished pouring a cup of hot coffee into his I HATE MONDAYS mug. He was dressed in a white button-down shirt, grey slacks and a silk tie which was now absorbing a new decoration while floating in the mug as he brought it to the kitchen table.

"Damn it," he cursed as he noticed it, then called to his wife. "Darlene."

The phone began to ring, and Darlene entered the kitchen in a hurry to answer it.

Richard continued to call her, ignorant to the ringing.

Darlene silenced him. "There's a clean one in the laundry room next to your blue slacks." Then she silenced the phone. "Hello?"

Richard followed his wife's directions and exited into the nearby laundry room.

Darlene was a typical, clean scrubbed midwestern housewife, modestly attractive. She bore little resemblance to her seventeen-year-old daughter, Rachel, but what the two did have in common, aside from good-looks, as Richard frequently pointed out, was gentle, compassionate eyes. Actually, Richard claimed that none of these traits were exactly hereditary; Darlene acquired her beauty from hanging around her husband for a long time, and Rachel . . . well, she was their daughter. Darlene always teasingly pushed him away whenever he joked around like that; a tradition he managed to keep alive within the Caruther household.

It was Rachel's turn to enter the kitchen, and the first thing she went for was the refrigerator; another daily tradition. She yanked open the door, peered inside for a moment, found what she wanted, and grabbed a carton of nonfat milk and a bagel.

Richard complained again from the laundry room. "Darlene, this tie has a spot on it. I can't wear this today! I have a ten-thirty with Chuck."

Into the phone, Darlene told Mrs. Pierce to hang on, then shouted, "Not *that* tie. On the other side. Look . . ." She spotted her daughter's breakfast. "That's not all you're eating, young lady."

"Oh. I found it, honey," Richard shouted back.

"Mom," Rachel explained, "I'm on a diet. You want an oinker for a daughter?"

Darlene sighed and returned to the phone. "Sorry," she said into the receiver, "do you think Susan could just bring her crutches? Stupid question. Tell her I hope she feels better. Yes. All right. That's fine. Good."

Behind her, Rachel popped the bagel into the microwave and set the timer. Richard reentered the kitchen, almost bumping into his daughter, working a windsor knot into his second silk tie. Darlene hung up the phone.

"Who's that, dear?" he asked her.

"Susan's mother. She can't baby-sit tonight."

He appeared half-surprised as he began to down a mouthful of his coffee. "Why not?"

"Susan broke her ankle last night at the ice rink. Rachel—"

Rachel had been attempting a soundless escape into the next room from the inevitability she sensed even as her mother had returned the receiver to its

45

cradle, her bagle still heating in the microwave. She halted at her mother's command.

"Mom, please."

"You have to watch Jamie tonight," she told her.

"I can't do it," Rachel complained. "Not tonight. You know I have this date with Brady. You know how important it is."

"Well tonight is very important to your father and me. This dinner party could set your father up for a much deserved promotion. You wouldn't want your date to mess that up, now would you?"

By this time, Richard had sat down to a warm plate of french toast, virtually ignoring the conversation, knowing his daughter had to succumb.

She persisted. "Can't you find somebody else?"

"It's too late," was the reply.

Silence, save for the ding of the microwave.

"What am I supposed to tell Brady?" Rachel said. "What am I supposed to say? 'Sorry, I've got to baby-sit my foster sister. Go have fun by yourself'?"

Darlene sighed. "It's not the end of the world, for goodness' sake."

"Sure it is," she argued. "I think tonight Brady was ready to make a commitment. Now my future relationship, engagement, marriage, children, and *your* grandchildren have all been wiped out, and all because *I have to baby-sit*. Oh joy."

Turning, Rachel nearly stepped into an apologetic Jamie. She was standing in the kitchen doorway, Sunday the labrador at her side.

Looking up at Rachel, she told her faintly, "I'm sorry I ruined everything. If I wasn't here, you could go out."

Then she turned and disappeared with Sunday into the livingroom around the corner. Rachel was left, staring guiltily into the empty space where the little girl had been. She could feel her parents' disapproving stares.

"Good job, Rachel," her father told her. "That little girl needs all the love we can give her, and all you can think about is yourself."

Without looking back, Rachel left the kitchen in pursuit of Jamie.

****

Rachel followed Jamie and Sunday into the girl's bedroom. Jamie didn't bother to close the door on her, but ignored her presence just the same by slipping onto her bed and pretending to toy with a pink marshmallow doll. Rachel joined her, sitting close. A moment of silence went by, Rachel trying to summon the right words to say to her, the words that best suited a six-year-old girl with a heavy heart. Finally, the words did come, and she hoped to God they would work.

"I'm sorry, Jamie. I didn't mean it like that. I can go out with Brady tomorrow night. No biggie."

Jamie remained preoccupied with her doll.

"Hey, come on," Rachel continued.

"But you wanted to go out tonight," Jamie responded softly. It was clear she was struggling to keep her voice calm. She was holding back tears, and being a real trooper at it, too. "It's my fault you can't."

Rachel had to think of something. Anything. "Well, tonight we're going to do something better. We're going to go trick-or-treating. How's that?"

"I don't want to."

"Okay." *Let's try something else.* "How about I pick you up from school this afternoon and we go for ice cream?"

That did it; Jamie just couldn't hold back that smile. There was something about little kids and ice cream, and Rachel had long since forgot what. Maybe it just tasted good.

"Double scoops?"

"Double scoops," Rachel said, and smiled back. *Thank God.*

Rachel gave her a big hug within the next instant, just as Sunday jumped up onto the bed. He was dying for a little love, too, and Rachel obliged him with a little scratch behind his ears. Then she stood up.

"Come on, kiddo. Let's get some breakfast."

Chapter Five

After driving for a few miles off the interstate, surrounded by nothing but desolation incarnated as dust and brambles and tumbleweeds rolling in the warm breeze as he passed, Doctor Loomis came upon a single roadside gas station/cafe. As he pulled up to the unleaded fuel pumps and stepped out of the sedan, he discovered the place was just as desolate and weatherworn as the miles of wasteland surrounding him. There didn't appear to be a soul around, and Loomis at first suspected whoever was here were all inside, or his presence would summon someone, an attendant most likely, and everything would be fine.

But everything wasn't fine. He sensed it as soon as his shoes met the dusty asphalt.

Nevertheless, he proceeded to fill up the sedan's tank with gas. As he did, he surveyed the area. Still no one came out to assist him. No one came out for any reason.

There was a vacant lot next door; nothing but a chainlink fence surrounding the same desert inside as there was outside. He expected there to be a dog of some sort within the boundaries of the fence, but as he gazed closer, his eyes momentarily blinded by the sun, he saw nothing.

Behind him stood a two door mechanic's garage, one door was open, disclosing a racked, weather-beaten blue Ford pickup truck, the long, rectangular window on the other door revealed nothing but darkness. Still, there was no movement save for the rustling of papers within the left garage, and the steady *rap rap rap* of what the doctor presumed to be a remote screen door on the other side, loosened by the wind.

The gas pump nozzle clicked off; he was finished pumping gas. The meter read nine dollars, and the doctor counted the money in his wallet and drew out a ten. He proceeded toward the open garage.

Still, there was no one in sight.

He halted. There was movement, behind the Ford.

"Hello," he called out. He waited.

There was no answer.

He must have been seeing things in the garage; for as he carefully peered inside, he found that no one was there. The wind gently swept through the garage's interior, rustling block and tackle chains hanging to his right on a wooden beam.

"Hello?" he called out again, this time louder.

Still not a soul.

Cautiously, he stepped past the Ford and into the shadows, eyes searching, finding a glass doorway at the end of a row of tool-lined shelving.

He called out a third time. "I said, hello. Is there anyone here?"

His gaze went to the opening of the garage, out into the area of the pumps where his sedan rested. He turned, and suddenly his face knocked dead center into dangling human legs and feet. Frantically, Loomis fought blindly at whatever was before him, arms waving impulsively, until he stumbled back and beheld what was hanging before him.

It was a body; nude, hanging among the block and tackle chains, motionless—pale.

Dear Jesus.

He stared upon the corpse, himself motionless, stunned—disbelieving. There was silence again, silence save for the steady creaking of the wood-beams from the body's weight as it slowly rotated above.

Loomis began to regain his footing; he was shaking from the sudden shock. He quickly exited the garage and entered through the glass double doors of the cafe. A door chime announced his panicked entrance, and he staggered over to the edge of the counter, gasping. He found the diner was just as deserted as it had appeared on the outside. There was a long line of empty booths and tables, and the counter was empty save for unfinished portions of breakfast on white plates.

People had been there. But what happened to

them. Well, that was something Loomis intensely feared.

A Hank Williams tune was sounding forth from an old transistor radio behind the counter. Loomis moved forward toward its direction, quietly and heedfully.

"Is anyone here?"

It took another step for him to see the waitress, stretched out across the floor, obviously strangled, cold eyes staring thoughtlessly into nothingness.

"God in heaven."

Loomis stepped back again, his feet faltering and causing him almost to stumble backwards, his hand brushing against the cash register at his side. The machine clamoured, and this startled him even further, causing him to jump. His breath was heavy. His hand reached for his chest, his heart pounding rapidly, and he felt that at any time it would beat its way out of his body, striking the inner reaches of his chest cavity until it was free, finally to silence. Another thought: perhaps, at the slightest wrong turn, at any given moment, someone else would do it for him.

Somehow he knew.

Someone he feared.

Once, five years ago, a patient had become hysterical in a psychiatric ward and hurled himself at the doctor. He had no other choice than to use his cane in self defense. It had become a sort of impulse. He realized he had left his cane in the sedan. No matter.

In his coat pocket was a gun, a nickle-plated,

9mm Smith and Wesson. He pulled it out. For what he was up against, what he feared was still there, perhaps in that very diner, he knew that this gun would prove just as useless as the cane. His eyes searched for the slightest movement—ears for the softest sound. His hands were shaking as he held the gun, unsure as to whether he would be quick enough if he came in contact with . . .

A telephone. There was a telephone under the counter. A trembling hand felt for it, his eyes never leaving the area before him. Then he looked down and saw to his disappointment that the receiver had been crushed. It was as if someone had simply lifted it and broke it within his grasp.

Damnit!

Just then, out of the corner of his eye, he thought he saw something. A figure. It was standing at the diner's far end in the shadows. Loomis swung around, pointing the gun feverishly.

There was no one there.

A door stood opened where he thought the figure had been. There was a sign indicating with a red arrow where the restrooms were. Another sign indicating public telephones. A silent video game with a cardboard sign taped over the coin slots reading OUT OF ORDER.

Blinking, Loomis crossed over to the open door. Carefully, he peered inside and discovered a dimly lit hallway leading into a series of back rooms, two of which were marked WOMEN'S and MEN'S. Mounted onto the wall across from them to the right were two pay phones, the receivers torn away.

Frustrated, the doctor turned and stepped back into the main room. What he saw made him freeze. Terrified, he could say nothing; he barely let out a single breath, his heart nearly ceased its frantic beating.

There It was.

It was just standing there, motionless, occupying the space where the body of the strangled waitress lay; where Doctor Loomis had been only a few minutes before. Hospital gown now absent, the shape wore mechanic's coveralls. His face was shadowed, yet Loomis could feel his cold gaze— that awful, hideous gaze.

Loomis held his gun up at eye level, attempting relentlessly to aim, his finger trembling against the trigger, his arms far from rigid.

Silence.

Then, finally, Loomis spoke. *"Why now?"*

No answer.

Loomis continued, a nervousness in his voice. "You've waited ten years. I told them to let you burn. I knew this day would come."

The shape stood, remaining there, silent and still. The diner was so incredibly tomblike at that moment the doctor could detect the figure's steady, oppressive breathing, even from his distance.

"Don't go to Haddonfield," Loomis demanded, lowering his gun. "If you want another victim, take me. But leave those people in peace."

Yet another moment of silence. Then, finally the dark shape turned and walked away toward the door of the kitchen.

At once, Loomis again raised his gun.

"Goddamn you, Michael!"

The overwhelming silence of the diner was interrupted by the booming thunder of three rapid shots. Michael was down, fallen behind the counter.

Loomis waited.

Nothing.

Quickly, he raced over to the counter. Brushing aside dishes and glassware, he cautiously leaned over the side.

Michael was gone; there was only the body of the waitress.

His first impulse was to continue into the kitchen itself, as this was the only direction Michael could have gone to. Still, he would have heard something; a shuffling, perhaps. It was as if the thing could disappear and reappear at will; as if he were a ghost. But the bodies were evidence he was no ghost. His second impulse was simply to turn and get the hell out of there, and he did so without further hesitation.

Outside in the warm breeze, he walked across the dusty expanse, the sounds of his soles on grit echoing throughout until they met the asphalt across which stood the service pumps and his sedan. His eyes scanned around, behind him and to his sides, expecting to see something, waiting for something to happen. The mechanic's garage was nothing but a shadowy cavern. Thoughts swept through Loomis' mind, making him paranoid to his circumstances. The figure could suddenly appear from the mouth of the garage, or surprise him from behind. What a wonderful trick-or-treat that would prove to be. Or he could be—did he leave his car unlocked? Yes, of course he did. As he drew closer to it, he slowly raised his gun, knowing, however, it would most likely do him no good.

Suddenly there was a sound; it came from behind him. It was the sound of a car door slamming. He turned. It came from the garage, echoing, ringing in his ear, then—silence.

"Michael!" he called out amidst the quiet. His voice joined the echo of the car door in a reverberating dance with the flurry of the wind. His gaze went to the side of the building, the space between the chain link fence.

Suddenly, Loomis pivoted back to the front of the garage as the boisterous sounds of a truck engine emanated from within the garage on the right. Loomis plummeted out of the way as the tow truck burst through the closed door of the right garage. Glass and wood splinters flew in the truck's wake, taking to the air and hurtling in every direction, some soaring into the doctor's side, sending him headfirst into the gravel in a space near the chain link fence.

There was no time to lie there. There was no time to be stunned like a rabbit in shock. The doctor scrambled to his feet and ran, just as the truck thunderously collided into the station's fuel pumps and in turn crashing into the Ridgemont sedan, octane spewing forth from all directions, sparks spreading through the air like fireworks. Occasionally turning back to witness the violent swamp of flames, Loomis continued to run. Suddenly the pumps exploded into a brilliant, burning flash of black and luminous orange, flames scorching and consuming the ruptured housing of the garage and adjoining diner. In turn, the underground tanks began to detonate, the destruction rocking the surrounding ground with force of an earthquake. The sedan burst into flames.

Loomis fell to his knees. He gazed up in the direction of the catastrophe, an arm flung up helplessly against the brilliant flashes, shielding his eyes; he attempted to shut himself out from the deafening flame roar and the concussive explosions shattering the remainder of the diner, first blowing out the windows, then in turn bringing the entire foundation to instant ruin. Meteors of wood showered in fragments around him, and he managed a feeble barrier around his head and face with his coat. He brought the coat down from his eyes, his face pasty white with fear. Intense fear. His body racked with shivers. Suddenly he was no longer bent over in the dust . . .

. . . he was no longer bent over . . .

. . . there was no longer any dust . . .

. . . there was just simply . . .

Flames, intense, burning flames . . .

and he could smell the charred flesh . . . his own charred flesh, as the men in long heavy coats surrounded him, working over heaps of fire, and for a moment he swore he was . . .

In hell. Oh, Jesus. Oh, God, I'm in *hell* . . . *in hell* . . .

and as they pulled him out, he was still burning, helplessly burning . . .

. . . and then he was back again, back in the surrounding dust and debris, but he could still hear voices. At first he could not recognize the voices, but then his mind somehow blotted out the rest, and he could hear something familiar, something crying out relentlessly . . .

. . . *don't save him, for chrissakes, don't.*

And he realized to his horror that it was *his* voice he was hearing, his voice long ago; his memories, distant and remote.

But the flames were there, the flames of the present; the dust was there, staining his face and hands. Yards away, a telephone line junction pole burned, its base shattered by the explosion. Suddenly, the entire pole toppled over, away from the exhausted and terrified doctor. Phone lines began to rip loose and dangle, spurts of electricity danced and quivered on asphalt and gravel.

The tow truck was nowhere in sight; but for that matter, Loomis didn't bother to look. He knew where It was headed. He knew what would happen tonight.

As he sat up, he rubbed his eyes from the momentary blindness caused by the intensity of the burning fumes and the smoke. Then he stood up. Determined, he walked in the direction of Haddonfield.

He knew what he must do. He knew what *someone* must do. Anyone. For if the police and the people from Smith's Grove or Ridgemont do nothing, blinded by their own absurdities and their own discernment, the town of Haddonfield would see a horror the likes of which no one had seen in *ten* years, because this time the horror would be much greater.

Michael Myers would return to his home town.

And tonight, this night, was Halloween.

Chapter Six

A bell sounded the anticipated ending of another tedious day of elementary school, and the many anxious children rushed from their classrooms and flooded the hallways with their presences and their shouts of laughter. They knew it was Halloween, and they knew that tonight they would once again get their bagfull of candy and neat-to-eat treats. They *should* be anxious; for this occasion only comes once a year to those fortunate enough to have costumes and participate in such a festive time of year.

Jamie, however, actually *was* fortunate, for every little tike her age who resided in Haddonfield had fortunate families to come home to. She just looked—well, she looked *odd*, being the only child in school without a Halloween costume to show off to her fellow classmates. Everyone else had some sort of outlandish costume; rarely did she spot someone with something ordinary or simple.

Most every child had a parent who was virtually an expert with needle and thread, or had a few extra bucks to spend for that extra set of clown shoes or those furry, floppy ears to make that Cocker Spaniel outfit look just right.

But noooo, Jamie didn't have a costume on, not so much as a mask, and it wasn't because her parents were poor or her mother didn't have time to sew anything together. It was simply because *she didn't want one*.

Now, there wasn't a sin in that; it wasn't a crime. But every other kid seemed to think so. Even that bratty little kid Kyle, the one with the clown suit with those stupid floppy shoes (couldn't he *trip* in shoes like that?), had to make her feel like she was committing a crime, and a real nasty one at that.

"Hey Jamie, where's your costume?"

She was just passing the playground, right near the monkey bars, on her way through the grass and headed out the chain link gate to the outside walkway. She turned and saw him. He was with a small band of cohorts and peers, and kids who simply came to watch little Jamie cry. It was like that, almost always. Almost.

"Where's your mask? Or are you wearing it?"

That was it; Jamie had to speak. "I don't need to wear a stupid costume."

Kyle teased, "That's because every day is Halloween at Jamie's house. Right, Jamie? Cause your uncle's the Boogeyman. Right, Jamie? Right, Jamie? Your uncle's the *Boogeyman*!"

In some ways, it was funny, all of them, dressed as clowns and bears and ghosts and buffalo. But to a little girl of six, it seemed like an abstract nightmare.

They all surrounded Jamie, resembling a childish imitation of a police brigade, except she didn't feel threatened by their presence as much as the words they chanted, repeating *Boogeyman, Boogeyman, Jamie's uncle's the Boogeyman. Boogeyman, Boogeyman JAMIE'S UNCLE'S THE BOOGEYMAN. BOOGEYMAN*.

Then a girl spoke out amongst them, "How come your mommy didn't make you a costume, Jamie?"

"How could she?" a boy responded. "Her mommy's *dead*!"

Suddenly the boy flashed a rubber skeleton straight into Jamie's face. At first she thought he was about to knock her down with it.

"Jamie's mommy's a *mummy*," Kyle continued to tease.

Impulsively, Jamie pushed her way through the band of children and managed to succeed in getting away from them. They began to chant once more.

JAMIE'S AN ORPHAN! JAMIE'S AN ORPHAN!

An orphan!

As the little girl stumbled her way through the remainder of the playground, her self-control gone wild as she sobbed and cried, she barely heard the rest of what they were saying, and didn't care who said it.

GO LIVE WITH YOUR BOOGEYMAN UN-CLE, JAMIE. WHEN YOU GROW UP, YOU CAN BE *JUST LIKE HIM*!!

And, between her sobbing, Jamie cried back, unaware that they could not hear her, "Stop it. Please, please stop it."

She continued to run. She ran out the gate, to the walkway and down a narrow asphalt driveway past a few parked cars, a parked stationwagon and out onto the neighborhood sidewalk, out of the sight of her tormentors. Had they followed? She turned, but could see no one. She hurried toward a patch of grass in front of a large home, and leaned against the maple tree there, exhausted and frightened. She tried to compose herself, as her mother taught her to do before she . . .

Her real mother.

She tried to force those thoughts from her head, from her memory, and, very slowly, she managed to succeed as best as she could. She told herself to be calm. *Just be calm. Everything will be all right*.

There it went again, the voice of her mother. The voice of Laurie Strode. It was useless.

She wiped the tears from her eyes, sniffing, and as she did so she began walking again. It didn't matter *where* she walked; all that truly mattered was the distance she put between her and those children somewhere behind her. Just to be sure, she glanced behind her again. No, they weren't there. But they would eventually show if she remained.

She continued walking, past driveways and green

lawns littered with deadened leaves, past other children engaged in eating some early Halloween candy and giggling to themselves about some inane joke.

Just then a dark brown sedan pulled up in front of her as she approached a remote intersection, the driver rolling down her window. Jamie thought she recognized the girl, and then Rachel leaned over the driver and began to wave.

"Hi, Jamie!"

Surprised, Jamie stepped over to the car. Rachel immediately sensed something in the girl's eyes and stepped out of the car, coming around the front and walking up to her. The closer she came, the more obvious were Jamie's tear reddened eyes.

"Jamie," she asked, concerned, "are you okay?"

Jamie forced a smile. "Yeah, I'm—"

For the moment, Rachel seemed to accept Jamie's halting answer and took her hand. Together, they hopped inside the sedan, Jamie squeezed between the two teenagers. The girl at the steering wheel pulled the car away from the curb.

"Jamie," Rachel said, referring to the other girl, "you remember Lyndsey, don't you?"

Lyndsey glanced down at the little girl. "Hi, Jamie."

"Hi," Jamie said back, shyly.

"Well, kiddo," Rachel asked her. "You ready for some ice cream?"

"I want to get a costume and go trick-or-treating—like the other kids," she replied.

Rachel was half-stunned; pleasantly surprised.

"But I thought you didn't want to go trick-or-treating."

Jamie said, nearly pleading, "Can't a girl change her mind?"

Lyndsey let out a brief chuckle.

Rachel smiled and accompanied Lyndsey with giggles of her own, inching towards the little girl. "I guess she can if she's as cute and ticklish as you are!"

And with that, Rachel's fingers managed to catch her foster sister's underarms and began to fiendishly tickle, while Jamie squealed and squirmed in her seat.

Among the childish uproar, and after a few final giggles from herself, Lyndsey spoke up casually as she made a left-hand turn at the intersection, "You know, Rach, the discount Mart's having a sale on Halloween costumes."

Sly, Lynd, real sly.

"Brady's working there today till six o'clock," Rachel told her, knowing that was the reason behind the suggestion.

"I know," Lyndsey said, confirming Rachel's thoughts. "Don't you want to talk to him?"

Yes you do, Rach. You gotta admit it.

"I don't want to look pushy," she replied.

"You won't look pushy."

"I don't want to come on too strong," she said. "Guys hate girls who come on too strong. Fragile egos and all that."

"You won't come on too strong," Lyndsey repeated.

"I don't want to seem desperate or anything."

"Face it, Rach. You are desperate."

Right you are. It can't be denied. The way Lyndsey glanced at her helped to apply the conviction.

"No, seriously," Lyndsey continued. "You're just going in to buy a costume for Jamie. Perfectly legit."

Rachel sighed. "I don't know."

Lyndsey impatiently awaited a definite answer. "Well, do I drop you at the Discount Mart, or do I drop you off at the Dairy Queen? Which is it?"

Rachel realized she must first ask the girl who actually started the whole predicament. "Jamie?"

"The Discount Mart," Jamie said. Then, "Can we get ice cream after?"

"You bet," Rachel said.

Another turn to the left, and the sedan went in the direction of a series of apartments, after which was a shopping district.

They didn't notice the tow truck idling at the intersection a block away.

Chapter Seven

It was afternoon and it was hot. To Doctor Loomis it was as hot as hell compared to before, with the exception of the magnitude of temperature in what he had witnessed earlier that morning.

He had been out there—what was it—five, maybe six hours? He had lost track of the time, merely guessing at when he had departed from the smoldering station and diner. He was walking up the road in the breakdown lane, and he realized as he went that if he kept an even, languid pace, he seemed to be all right; if he walked too fast, he would stagger and fall. He had found that out the hard way a few miles back, when he staggered and hit his head on the asphalt. No damage done, though. At least none that he knew of. Hell, he'd been through worse.

The distant sound of a motor engine. He turned and spotted the station wagon; yes, it was a beige station wagon, and there appeared to be a family inside, a family with children. They looked like the kind of people who would help a desperate man in the middle of scorching desert. He could cast aside his fear of being picked up by a gay rapist or a drug dealer ex-con.

He held out his thumb. It didn't look like the station wagon was going to stop.

It didn't.

Well, so much for that.

He came across a road sign:

EATON, Ill. 59mi.

HADDONFIELD, Ill. 119mi.

Suddenly, another car engine echoed down the road; the engine of a red and white convertible. This time, the car slowed, veering over to the shoulder about fifty feet ahead. The car was filled with teenagers, and from the looks of them they were returning from a high school football game. Two girls, cheerleaders complete in skimpy yellow and black outfits with megaphone patches across their chests began to wave him towards the car.

Thank God.

"Thank you," Loomis called out to them, trotting towards the vehicle, ". . . thank you for stopping . . ."

Just as he came up to the car, barely close enough to touch it, the rear wheels began to spin, spraying a roostertail of dust into the air around the doctor. The teenagers gave a hearty laugh as they drove away, up the road and off into the distance. Loomis was left alone, angrily beating the dirt from his clothes and the coat he carried over one arm.

As he looked up the road he noticed what appeared to be a beat-up old pickup waiting in the center of the asphalt up ahead. An older man lifted his head out from the driver's side window and yelled to him.

"Get it in gear, old man, I ain't got till Judgment Day."

Loomis approached the vehicle, walking a bit too fast and almost staggering, until he came up to the passenger's side, opened it, and climbed inside.

"Thank you," he told the driver gratefully, panting, still unconsciously wiping dust from his shirt.

"Anything for a fellow pilgrim," the old man replied. "We're all on a quest. Sometimes we need help getting where we got to be. Milk Dud?"

"Excuse me?" Loomis saw the small yellow box in the man's hand, and shook his head politely.

Occasionally, Loomis would glance at the old man, each glance revealing something different and curious. He appeared to be in his late sixties, with wheat textured tufts of whiskers and scalp hair. The man wore a preacher's collar around his neck, and he was holding a fifth of corn whiskey in each hand, one appearing as if he were on the verge of spilling it as he steered. And his name was . . .

"Jack Sayer. Just a pilgrim trodding this here Earth in the guise of an old country preacher tryin' to save a few poor damn bastards from takin' a dive into hell. And you?"

"Uh, Loomis. Doctor Sam Loomis."

Sayer motioned to shake his hand, then declined, not knowing where to rest the corn whiskey. Loomis felt slightly uncomfortable, and at first he feared the man would run the truck off the road at any moment; but it was a fear that subsided as the miles steadily went by. The man was definitely a preacher. A crucifix hung from his rear view mirror like a guardian angel. Dangling by invisible fishing line, it appeared to be floating rather than hanging suspended. There was a Gideon bible on the dashboard near a small box of tissues.

A moment of quiet passed, the man apparently in thought. "Yeah, you're huntin' It all right. Just like me."

Loomis looked at him. "What are you hunting, Mister Sayer?"

"Apocalypse. End of the world. Armageddon. It's always got a face and a name." He took a slow, easy drink of his whiskey. "Been huntin' the bastard for thirty years give or take. Come close a time or two. Too damn close."

Loomis studied Sayer for a second, detecting a certain sincere firmness in his voice. Sayer glanced back at him, and in his long glance he appeared sober as a judge.

Then Sayer said to him, "Can't kill damnation, mister. It don't die like a man dies."

"I know," Loomis told him, speaking from experience.

"You're a pilgrim," Sayer said. "I seen it in your face back there in the dust. I seen it clear as breasts and blue suede shoes. Drink?"

At first the doctor's impulse was to decline, then, he figured, on second thought, he might as well. Jack Sayer handed him one of his fifths, and, hesitatingly, he managed a sip. The old man flipped on the A.M. radio to an all gospel station and began to sing along with an unseen choir at the top of his lungs, proudly but off key.

When the roll . . . is called up yonder, when the roll . . . is called up yonder, when the roll . . . is called up yonder, when the roll is called up yonder I'll be there . . .

Loomis gazed out the window, his thoughts wandering while the old man missed all the right notes.

Chapter Eight

Doctor Hoffman had been dialing his desk phone for centuries. At least, it certainly seemed like that long. He sat there, in his office, and he knew he had much paperwork to get finished for the next day: reports; receipts for new equipment needed to be handled; there were some tax papers needing to be looked at; and, on top of it all he had personal business to attend to. But, try as he did, he could not manage to get his mind in focus. It was because of that damn Loomis. He hadn't heard from Loomis all day, and he had urgently called Haddonfield time and time again throughout the day, calling and fidgeting with his papers, calling and fidgeting.

But all he got was nothing.

Absolutely nothing.

His patience wearing thin, he tried once more. One final time. Frustrated, he listened to the same automatic voice reciting the same automatic lines:

"We're sorry, your call did not go through . . ."

He slammed the receiver down onto its cradle. Then he decided to dial the operator.

"Yes, operator, I've been trying to reach the police in Haddonfield off and on all day, and now it's become quite urgent—"

"I'm sorry," the voice rang through the receiver, "we're experiencing technical problems along our long distance lines."

"This is an emergency!"

"I suggest you try your call again in an hour."

Infuriated, the doctor slammed down the receiver once more, this time shoving the phone from his desk and onto the floor with a *clang*.

'Damn you, Loomis," he cursed. "Why did you have to be right."

Chapter Nine

"Make your move, Wade," Brady told him, provokingly.

Wade was hesitant. Actually, it was more than that; Wade was *nervously* hesitant. There was a difference. Looking back upon his friends with the distinct expression of someone asked to strip down to his balls in the center of the parking lot, he responded, "Don't rush me, Brady. The timing's got to be primo."

Brady in his dark blue sales clerk smock stood with his two friends, Wade and Tommy, conversing with them from behind a service counter. It was usual for them to visit him this time of day, and at times he thought it a bit weird for them to come into the store to talk to him only an hour after he started. But his boss didn't seem to mind, because it was at this particular time when business was slow, and he didn't have any other work to do, anyway. Besides, he was a *sales clerk*, and not a stock boy.

Then again, there was Kelly, who happened to be a sales clerk also (and an extremely attractive one at that), and *she* was busy at work stocking a series of racks with batteries two aisles down from a display of cheapo, half-priced watches. Nevertheless, since Brady had nothing whatsoever to do at the moment, he had taken up conversation with Wade and Tommy, the two eggheads that were always hot over Kelly. Perhaps *that* was why they always showed up at that time; not to see their good friend Brady, but to see the eighteen-year-old with the big batteries.

Wade didn't like to be rushed with these matters. *Of course* he wanted to ask Kelly out. What guy his age in their right mind wouldn't? A fool, that was for sure. A *damn* fool. But Wade was no damn fool; he just needed *time*. Tommy and Brady both just couldn't seem to understand that, and both of them had better chances at her than he did. Hell, plenty of girls eyed Brady every day, with his cute features. *Come on, Wade, admit it. Brady was cute and ol' Wade just wasn't. He hated that word, CUTE. It was something girls had an affinity for. That word.*

Then again, maybe he hated that word because nobody ever said that about him.

He looked at Brady, irascibly. "I don't see you asking her out. You got the best chance."

"You're the jock," Brady responded.

Yes, it was true, Wade was a jock, but buff guys in the world of jocks do not necessarily have tickets to the Game of Getting Women. Well, Wade wasn't an *unattractive* jock.

"Jock itch, maybe," Tommy jested.

Wade resented that. "Shut up, assface."

Tommy continued, "You don't have the guts God gave a cockroach and you know it."

"Don't bet on it," Wade said back.

It was Brady's turn. "Money talks, Wade. Bullshit walks."

There we go: Tommy's digging in his pocket for money again. He's always one for bets.

Tommy slammed a ten-dollar bill down onto the service counter. "Double or nothing you won't ask Kelly out."

He saw in his eyes that Wade was actually going to go through with it.

"Don't forget," Brady warned, "she's Sheriff Meeker's daughter. Remember Reed Collins?"

"Yeah," Tommy recalled. "Meeker made Reed wear his balls for a bowtie."

Wade *was* going to go through with it. He dug from his pocket a wad of bills, counted out ten ones, and placed them on the counter on top of Tommy's ten.

"Sheriff don't scare me," he declared. "I'm gonna nail his little girl right in the trophy room of that big old white elephant of a house."

"Screw you," Tommy taunted.

And, as if to say the same, Wade walked down past the rest of the counters, turned, and advanced toward Kelly. She was still in the process of placing the batteries on the racks; she had started with the top row and worked her way to the bottom. As Wade approached she proceeded to do the bottom row, bending over, unknowingly inviting his hormones to react deliciously.

Wade slowed.

Her clothes were just tight enough, her body was sooo firm, and in all the right places.

Wade stood there, having inched his way closer. He didn't bother to pull a glance at his friends, who were undoubtedly cracking jokes to themselves. They were just secretly jealous.

The young woman still didn't notice him; he certainly noticed *her*.

He cleared his throat.

"Nice try, Wade," she said, not looking up.

Wade was stunned.

Finally, she *did* look up, a consoling smile across her face. Maybe she pitied him. "But the answer's no. Sorry."

She returned to her work as if nothing happened.

Damn!

Wade turned and proceeded sheepishly towards the service counter once again, not wanting to have to face his so-called friends. He could see them laughing; hear their tormenting remarks. Being seventeen-years-old and with no girlfriend certainly sucked.

Tommy, of course, was the first one to speak. "You really nailed her."

"The timing was primo, man," Brady added.

Wade resented that. "Shut up."

Just then, Brady spotted something beyond

Tommy, who was beginning to bicker with Wade about who actually got the bet money. *I did ask her, you idiot, Wade would say; but you didn't get anywhere, would be Tommy's reply.*

But Brady was beyond them now, and he gave a look of surprise as his eyes met Rachel's coy smile. She had entered the store with her foster sister, Jamie.

"I thought I was picking you up?" he said.

Rachel told him casually, "Jamie needs a Halloween costume."

"End of aisle A," Brady directed. "Those are the best in the store. Actually, just about the best in *any* store here."

Jamie tugged at Rachel's belt. "Come look with me, Rachel."

"In a second," Rachel told her. Then she said to Brady, bluntly, "We have to talk."

"Sure," Brady blinked. "About what?"

Brady and Rachel separated themselves from Jamie, and Jamie took this as a hint to go look at the costumes by herself. Actually, she'd much rather Rachels' company, but she was delighted just the same to get to where she wanted, passing Wade and Tommy who were adjourning to the magazine racks, past rows of bagged candy and boxed chocolate bars; she turned to the aisle over which hung a large red "A", and entered. There they were, to the left and to the right of her, oodles upon oodles of them: Halloween costumes.

Tons of them. Loads of them. Masks and capes and clown noses and clown wigs. Cardboard skel-

81

etons, vampire teeth and tubes of fake vampire blood, rubber witches on brooms, and, as she walked further on, there were entire outfits with colorful arrangements of plastic masks with rubber bands and thin, plastic body suits.

****

Brady led Rachel to an aisle on the far side of the store where there were no customers or employees, and it was there they commenced with whatever conversation Rachel was going to begin.

Instead of coversation, Brady slowly pulled Rachel close and into a tender kiss; warm, compassionate. And she accepted this kiss fully, embracing. But this was no time to remain compassionate. Not now. Rachel broke away.

Brady knew what was to happen next. "It's about tonight."

It was time to talk, regretfully.

"My parents' baby-sitter cancelled," she admitted, not wanting to.

"So?"

"So, I have to watch Jamie tonight."

This wasn't fair. "When did you find out?"

"This morning."

Now he was upset. "And you're just telling me now. Christ, it's after five o'clock! Why in the hell didn't you call earlier?"

Rachel was upset right along with him, knowing he would be this way. But, unlike him, she held it all in. Or, at least, she tried to. "Don't get angry."

"I'm *not* angry!" he half-yelled. Then, finally, he *did* manage to compose himself. "Why don't I come over after Jamie goes to bed?"

"My parents won't be home."

"Good."

After a moment, after Rachel had time to swallow this idea, she became tense, uncomfortable. "I don't know, Brady. My parents . . ."

Exhaling frustration, Brady turned to get back to whatever work he was doing. As he did so, he spotted Kelly at the end of the aisle. She'd been watching them, maybe even listening, and offered him an alluring smile before she disappeared down the way. Just then, something echoed through his mind; something Wade had said.

I don't see you asking her out. You got the best chance.

No. There was Rachel.

But you got the best chance . . .

But then, perhaps by his will, the voice faded.

****

Jamie stood at the rack of costumes, looking each one over carefully. Well, almost each one; there were so many.

There, she thought, *this one . . . I like this one.*

Beyond the wolf man, between the Casper and the Ronald Reagan, was a clown outfit. She pulled it out.

There was something interesting about this particular clown suit; something reminiscent. Some-

83

thing vaguely familiar. It was red on one side and silvery white on the other, pompom-like buttons trailing down the middle and voluminous, white nylon ruffles about the collar. Removing it from its hanger, she looked around for a mirror. There was one down the way near the wall. She walked up to it and stood there, holding the costume out before her at first, admiring it.

"Rachel," she called out, "I found the perfect costume. Come see."

She held the clown costume up to herself and gazed into the mirror, imagining how nice it would be, how splendid it would look when she wore it. Then Kyle and the other kids wouldn't talk; they would see how wonderful her new clown costume was, and they wouldn't say anything. They would just leave her alone, for once. Perhaps they wouldn't even recognize her in this outfit, partly because they wouldn't expect her to be wearing one, so they wouldn't mention Uncle Michael, too. They wouldn't say anything about . . .

Oh my God.

Her reflection in the mirror had changed. Was this an illusion? Yes; now it was gone. She thought for a moment that she was no longer gazing into the mirror at herself. It was . . . the image of a boy . . . a boy wearing *her* clown costume. He had a knife, a butcher knife, and he . . . he was grinning back at her, grinning mindlessly, as if there were no real thoughts behind that grin; as if the grinning were only a reflex from the evil . . .

Startled, Jamie blinked and stepped away from

the mirror, unbelieving. Alarmed, she turned and began to run, but the legs of the shape she thudded into made her halt. She gazed up to his face at the precise moment the dark figure slipped a pasty white Halloween mask over his features.

She was stunned, and for a second her mind was having difficulty perceiving. "Uncle Michael?"

Silently tilting his head downwards, the shape's bulky hands came together and started for her. Once again she turned, slamming headfirst into the mirror behind her. The mirror shattered, perhaps knocking her senses back into reality, a reality where she *knew* this was actually happening, that somehow, by some means she knew only within the boundaries of nightmares, her uncle was truly there and was truly attempting to take her life. She screamed. Splintered shards crashed and spun across the hard tile floor, and she nearly slipped on them; and had she attempted to run any further she most likely would have, except she saw Rachel and Brady. They were running up to her from the other end of the aisle. She hadn't realized it just then, but she hadn't seen Rachel ever look so seriously worried.

The two ran for each other, Rachel knocking over a rack of children's books in the process. Rachel grabbed her foster sister and held her close, feeling her tremble in her arms.

"Jamie," she said, "what happened?"

Jamie began to sob weakly. "It was the nightmare man."

"What?"

85

"He's . . . he's come to get me, Rachel."

Brady stood there, not knowing what to do. He was soon joined by his two friends, who gazed around at the shattered glass.

"Shhhhh," Rachel consoled her. "You're okay. You probably saw a mask and it scared you. At least you're not cut." She double-checked Jamie's features to make sure. Satisfied, she said, "Come on, let's go home."

"You said ice cream," Jamie said, rubbing her eyes innocently.

"Ice cream," she remembered, "I didn't forget."

"Busted mirror," Wade commented. "Seven years bad luck."

"Shut up, butthead," Tommy said.

And as they began to escort the two girls out to the front of the store, none of them saw the shape, his reflections staring blankly from the dozens of shards of glass amidst the masks and some stray children's books.

****

"Better?" Rachel asked Jamie.

"Yeah."

The sun prepared to set upon the two girls strolling down the sidewalk; they each carried double-scoop cones of ice cream, their long shadows accompanying them as they went.

"Ready for tonight?" Rachel said.

Jamie smiled expectantly. "I'll get lots of candy?"

"Lots," she answered. "But let Mom go through it first. Sometimes people play mean tricks on kids."

"Your mom's real nice, Rachel."

"She's your mom, too. And pretty soon, who knows, maybe my parents'll make it legal."

Casually and happily, Jamie continued to lick her cone until she caught sight of something ahead suddenly, and she froze in her tracks.

Up at the end of the block, standing partially within the shade of the tree on the front lawn of the corner house, was the Shape, the dark man; the one she ran into unexpectantly at the Discount Mart. The one she didn't quite frankly want to run into ever again.

It was the nightmare man.

It was Uncle Michael.

Rachel turned and looked at her. "What's the matter?"

"It's him," Jamie all but whispered.

Rachel was confused. "Who?"

She turned only to see an empty distant shadow beside the corner house. At least, that was where Jamie seemed to be casting her fearful gaze. Rachel looked around; there were only a few children Jamie's age walking on the opposite side of the street, and a Plymouth passed them by.

Nothing more.

"The nightmare man," Jamie answered, still staring. There was this distant, far-away stare deep within her eyes, as if she were entranced; Rachel also noticed a certain shade of terror within that look. Or was it momentary shock? Regardless, Rachel was concerned. "He was next to that house."

There was no one there *now*.

"I'll go look, okay?" Rachel told her, to which the little girl didn't at first reply.

Then, as Rachel proceeded to walk over to the shadows, Jamie cried out diffidently, "Rachel. Don't."

But Rachel continued; and as she did so, she stepped around the edge of the corner house and out of view.

Long seconds passed; too long for Jamie. Her worry ached within her, growing into an irrepressible panic.

Now Rachel had joined the shape's absence.

"Rachel?" Jamie called out.

Nothing.

"Rachel!" she repeated, yelling.

Her ice cream cone slipped from her fingers and dropped upside down on the sidewalk. She ran— ran to the front lawn of the house at the corner, ran right through the shade of the tree, crushing multitudinous fallen leaves, stamping through a wide river of water formed by a water hose stretched across the darkened grass—ran until she arrived at the other side.

No Rachel.

There was a white wooden fence that ran along the edge of the house until it gave way to a separate wall crawling with English ivy. She called out again for her foster sister.

"Rachel, are you all right?"

And around the other side of the ivy covered wall, a middle-aged German Shepherd, startled, began to lunge at her; held back only by the length of its chain. Jamie jumped backwards as the dog barked and snarled . . . backed right up into a figure.

She screamed.

"No nightmare man," Rachel told her. "Just your imagination."

Chapter Ten

Twilight rose with the new moon and cast its dim light upon the first evening trick-or-treaters on their quest for the very things their mothers had always said would make their teeth fall out. At times, one could see some of these very mothers accompanying their children out on the nighttime sidewalks, but for the most part, a majority of the children's overseers were fathers or big brothers and sisters.

The tranquil silence of Autumn gave way to an evening of festivity, a tradition the likes of which Haddonfield, along with the rest of the country, had seen year after anticipated year. Actually, however, no one really anticipated Halloween; at least not as much as most other holidays. Halloween just *arrived*. Sure, as the days grew closer to October thirty-first, the children grew more excited and the parents made ready the costumes and the churches began to spread flyers about their Fall festivals and hay rides, but it just seemed to come naturally. Not like Christmas, surrounded by all the hustle and bustle of shopping and tree decorating and whatnot. Then again, Halloween, when it finally arrived, *did* have its own, very unique magical properties as do all holidays. Tonight was no exception to that magic.

But sometimes that magic can be deadly.

He was watching. He was watching those children, watching as they strode from house to house with their plastic bags or paper bags or plastic jack-o-lanterns. He saw how protecting their guardians were; their mothers or fathers, friends or relatives making sure they got their kids back from each stop, keeping them all out of trouble.

They did not see him; he stood perfectly still, like the Caruthers' willow tree beside him. If anyone *did* see him, they must have paid no attention to him. It was Halloween, and strange sights or absurdities were overlooked tonight. Besides, how absurd can a simple man in a mask standing beside a tree *be*? But standing within the shadows as he was, one terrible aspect was certain: *he could see them better than they could see him*.

He was no longer beneath the willow. He reappeared beside the Caruthers' kitchen window, gazing inside, upon the teenage girl clearing a table full of the evening's dinner dishes. And there was the little girl; she was helping the older one by stacking the rinsed plates inside the dishwasher.

Darlene and Richard entered the kitchen, and Rachel was the first one to see them garbed in their party outfits. They looked splended, Rachel thought. Dad in his tux and Mom in a pink and white ruffled froufrou dress. They appeared elegant together, and by the look in Jamie's eyes as she turned also, she agreed. Now, to Rachel, they would look even more elegant out the door.

"All right," Darlene told them both, "we're leaving. How do we look?"

"Elegant," Rachel said. "You guys always look great."

"We'll be at the Fallbrooks," her mother told her. "The number is next to the phone."

Rachel hated this part of babysitting . . . the beginning lecture. "I know. Next to that is the Police, hospital, fire, and probably the National Guard."

The last of the dishes within the dishwasher, Jamie accompanied her foster family to the front door, and Mr. and Mrs. Caruthers exchanged her kisses. Then she darted up the staircase to where a clown costume was waiting for her in her bedroom.

"Have a good time tonight, you two," Richard told them as Jamie disappeared. Then, to Rachel, "Make sure Jamie's in bed by nine-thirty. No later."

Rachel was indeed right; they do look more elegant out the door. "You're going to be late. You don't want to blow your promotion."

"Don't make fun," Darlene said back. "Tonight is the difference between vacations in Bermuda and another two weeks visiting your grandmother in Cleveland."

"So hurry up," said Rachel.

And that is what her parents did. Rachel closed the front door and automatically went for the livingroom telephone.

Upstairs, Jamie busily brushed her teeth as she always had done every evening after dinner. Within her bedroom, down the hall past the master bedroom, Sunday moved cautiously toward the shadows beyond the open window. Suddenly he sensed something, and he backed up towards the open door. There was something there. A presence. A low growl swelled within his throat.

Something was in Jamie's room.

But when Jamie entered and flicked on the light switch, the light flooded over dozens of dolls and nothing else. Jamie thought the clown costume looked great on her; that it looked fantastic just like she knew it would. She gazed at it admiringly in the full-length mirror.

Downstairs, Rachel's voice echoed through the livingroom as she sat on the couch cross-legged. preoccupied with the extremely urgent business she needed to take care of over the telephone.

"Is Brady there?" she spoke casually but hopefully. "Has he come home from work yet? Okay. Well, when he does, tell him to drop by about eight. I'll be home by then. Okay? This is Rachel. Okay, bye."

Then, upon setting the receiver down upon its cradle, Rachel called out, "Come on, Jamie. Let's go. You're going to miss all the good candy!"

Jamie heard her calls. She set the mask over her

face, gazed at it for a moment, smiling, realizing that she *even looked way better than those stupid kids who made fun of her*.

Something distracted her. She turned toward the closet.

Didn't she hear the door creak? Was that coming from *her* room? Where was Sunday?

"Come on, kiddo," the call echoed from downstairs.

Nevermind.

She darted happily toward the voice of her foster sister.

But the shape had been watching, even as she admired her costume, and, in a way, he admired it too. From within the shadowy depths of the closet, he gazed down upon the opened box of memories. He lifted up pictures, photographs of days gone by, memories he shared unknowingly with the little girl, and memories only he alone could summon. He saw the woman Laurie Strode. A teenager. He saw the little girl with her father, posing with a barbecue in the background. And he saw himself, in the ever familiar clown costume, the one the little girl even now wore proudly, and he was standing next to his sister on that night so long ago yet so recent.

That night was here again.

Downstairs, Rachel was checking the stove burners in the kitchen. She grabbed her jacket on the rack near the front door and checked her pockets for the house keys. Finally satisfied, she turned to Jamie, who was coming down the stairway.

"I thought you were ready," Jamie said, observing Rachel slipping into her jacket and returning to the kitchen to turn off the lights.

"I'm ready," she replied. "I'm ready. Okay, let's go."

The shape at the top of the stairs watched silently, silent with the exception of the ragged breathing which seemed to reverberate through the darkness surrounding him, as the two girls disappeared out the door.

Back within the depths of the closet, the dog's low growls were forever stifled; it lay in a bloody heap, its neck broken and its' head hanging loosely over bloodstained rag dolls . . . silent, unmoving, its unseeing eyes gazing out into the horror it last beheld.

Forever gazing.

Chapter Eleven

The Haddonfield Sheriff's Department wasn't as large as it appeared to be on the outside. It was housed in a one story beige building with a medium sized parking lot accented with dozens of rows of junipers and a flower bed shared in part by the Haddonfield Public Library next door.

There was no such thing as sophistication when it came to a small town like Haddonfield, and small towns have small police forces. Of course, if anything unusual occurred, other departments would be notified, firstly the state police. But nothing unusual ever happened. For the most part.

The inside of the building was as bland as the outside, displaying such average sights as a copy machine (which was out of order for the time being, the employees having to go to the library next door for copies), bulletin boards, a gun rack situated near the back wall, a water cooler expecting a refill, desks and phones and a dart board near the back between the time clock and the single restroom. To complete the atmosphere, there was a threesome of deputies behind the desks, one of whom was conversing with his wife over the telephone—something about a hamster and a liquid cleanser and how a girl named Marsha should be spanked.

At the front desk, the deputy was occupying his own time by reading his favorite section from *Reader's Digest*, chuckling at the humorous anecdotes.

Suddenly, his attentions were distracted by a man who stormed into the building through the front glass double doors. The fellow appeared to be quite flustered, serious . . . determined, and immediately the deputy knew that this was definitely going to be *one of those nights*. The balding man, wearing a dark overcoat and a dusty outfit beneath, marched directly up to his desk.

"I need to see Sheriff Bracket," Doctor Loomis demanded.

The deputy set the open magazine face down on the green blotter before him, leaned back casually in his seat, and gave a hearty laugh. *Of course, this guy couldn't be serious.*

He told the man, "Then you need to travel 'bout three thousand miles south'a here."

Loomis was suddenly confused. "What?"

"Brackett retired in '81," the deputy informed him. "Up and moved to St. Petersburg. We get a postcard every Christmas."

"Well, who the hell is *the new sheriff?"*

"I am," spoke another voice. "Ben Meeker."

The doctor's gaze shot beyond the deputy and saw a husky, solid two hundred pound sheriff standing to the man's left. He had inquisitive yet hardened brown eyes and a brown crew cut, and by the look of his heightened stature he appeared to be over six feet tall. If people were cartoon animals, this man would have been a grizzly bear.

The doctor wasted no time. "Sheriff Meeker, My name's . . ."

"Loomis," Meeker finished for him. His voice was deep and commanding. "Folks around here aren't likely to forget *your* face. At least, not cops. What the hell brings you back here after ten years?"

He sounded resentful, but there was something within his tone that the doctor detected as weariness. "Michael Myers," he told him. "He's escaped Ridgemont. He's here in Haddonfield."

"That's impossible," Meeker said. "He's supposed to be an invalid."

But there was this seriousness in his eyes. "He's *here*, Sheriff."

Meeker was the kind of Sheriff who was known for possessing a very deep sense of humor. *Deep*, meaning that in order to be able to find it, you would have to dig *deep* into his personality. He took his job seriously, and even when the situation seemed too absurd to be true, he faithfully investigated; or he would send some deputy to do it for him, and the deputy would curse to himself for finding a dead gopher in the middle of the road instead of a dead baby, or an old man who insisted he saw Buddah staring at him from outside his bedroom window, like two weeks ago.

"Why would he be here?" he questioned.

Loomis told him sternly, "The car crash that killed Laurie Strode and her husband left an orphan in Haddonfield."

The Sheriff was plainly surprised. *"Jamie Lloyd?"*

"Yes. Wherever that child is, she's in *danger*."

Meeker was still inquisitive, his interests up. "Myers' been locked up since before she was born. He's never laid eyes on her."

"Six bodies, Sheriff," Loomis declared. "That's what I've seen between here and Ridgemont . . . a filling station in flames. Michael Myers is here in this town *right now! He's come to kill that child and whoever else stands in his way!*"

Meeker's lips drew thin. His eyes were hardened and pensive. He was contemplating.

Then, he turned to the deputy with the *Reader's Digest*. "Call the State troopers and check this story." He turned to Loomis, "All right, let's assume for a minute that what you say is true . . ."

"It *is* true, Sheriff!" he insisted as the deputy obeyed and began to dial.

The sheriff continued, "Fine. If it's true, then I want to know what the hell we can do to avoid a repeat of ten years ago."

"We have to find the little girl," Loomis instructed. "Get her someplace safe. Call the local tv. Tell them to get everyone off the streets and behind locked doors."

The deputy turned from the phone. "I can't get long distance, Sheriff. Operator says the phone lines are down."

This was cause enough for the sheriff to move. His tremendous build swerved around the convocation of desks until he came to the shotgun rack. He went immediately for a twelve guage Ithaca pump, and pulled it down. He knew his profession well; everything was automatic, flowing like clockwork as he loaded shells and pocketed anything remaining. He turned to Doctor Loomis, striding back toward the front desk.

"Coming?"

"Not until I see your man make that call."

The deputy began to dial at the sheriff's command, and, satisfied, Loomis, turned back to Meeker.

"All right," the sheriff told him, "let's go check on the girl."

As they started for the front double doors, they could hear the first few sentences of the deputy as he spoke into the receiver: "Yeah, Sheriff's office calling for Bill Miller . . . Bill, Deputy Pierce . . . We got an emergency situation here. We need everybody off the streets pronto . . ."

Chapter Twelve

Rachel swore to herself that she never had been as thoroughly excited about Halloween and trick-or-treating as Jamie was this night. Nearly every single time she visited the doorstep of some cheerful neighbor who smiled and said something sweet and dropped a few pieces of candy into her plastic bag, she would politely but hurryingly blurt out a 'thank you' and be well on her way to the next house, half-running. To Rachel, Halloween was fun, not in a strict sense but in a sort of sense that this night wasn't dull and ordinary. And, of course, she enjoyed the fact that Jamie was truly happy; overjoyed, even.

"Wait for me," Rachel called out, refusing to run. "Jamie, wait . . ."

But the little girl was too involved with the splendor of it all; her little clown outfit, sparkling dimly under the street lights, more and more small packages of chocolate and lemon drops and bubble gum waiting to fill her bag. "This is *great*, Rachel!"

The next door revealed an overweight, t-shirted fellow who held a can of beer in one hand and a handful of candy in the other. Alcohol undoubtedly blending his thoughts into a jelly of drowsiness, he nearly plopped the half-empty can into her sack before catching his actions and withdrawing, chuckling to himself. Jamie joined in the laughter and frolicked merrily away.

"Cute kid," the man remarked to no one, and closed the screen door.

The next house; this time it was a grey haired elderly woman who greeted her, an orange robe covering a pink nightgown. She appeared to be delighted before the little girl, and perhaps this was the reason her handful of candy was the most generous thus far.

"Trick or treat!" Jamie said, at the same time the lady held out the candy.

"My," the woman said, "what a cheery little clown. Look what I've got for you."

Jamie's eyes immediately lit up into a felicitous resplendence. "Thank you."

"You're very welcome, honey."

Jamie walked toward her foster sister, who was waiting on the sidewalk listening to the meager sizzling of the electric cables of the telephone poles above, her mind on the pleasantries of the remainder of the evening, back at home, Jamie asleep and Brady downstairs with her.

Jamie halted beside her for a moment, her fingers sifting through the bulk of her plastic jack-o-lantern/ghost bag.

Rachel looked down at her. "Had enough?"

"No way," Jamie said. She turned, and Rachel followed her past a series of hedges enroute to the next house. "Halloween is great. Can we stay out all night?"

"Forget it, kiddo. We're home by eight o'clock."

As they came upon the next house, the last house on the corner past the hedges, they saw that the porch light was off. Rachel told her to ignore the house; that the family living there was either sick or out somewhere on vacation or at a party. In Haddonfield, most everyone participated in one way or another in this particular holiday, unlike other cities Rachel had heard about where churches had condemned the celebrations as being paganistic and therefore sinful to practice. All Rachel knew was that tonight, in the world of the contemporary, all of the parties and bobbing for apples and putting on costumes and going door-to-door was as innocent as a newborn baby. She had many fond memories of the custom from her childhood, and Jamie and every other little girl or boy would not be the least bit harmed with the same fond memories.

Anyway, aside from what *other* people did or did not do on this night, Rachel knew that it was also a night for little, quiet get-togethers . . . get-togethers in livingrooms, *dark* livingrooms, maybe even dark *bedrooms* . . . while certain parents

were having a good time with their friends somewhere, too.

Rachel directed Jamie across the street to start
on another block, and when Rachel looked down
at her glow-in-the-dark Timex, she knew that this
block would be the last. As they arrived at the
other side, they came across a small group of
children who appeared to be around Jamie's age,
wearing brightly colored clown suits with awkward-
looking shoes and ghost white sheets and there
was even a kid with a huge, plastic buffalo head
which forced him to hang his bag of candy by a
string around his neck in better effort to hold up
the monstrosity. They looked like refugees from a
Saturday morning cartoon nobody wanted to view.
The one with the stupid floppy shoes, the clown
with the stripes as if posing as an escaped convict
from the circus, went up to Jamie.

"Wow!" Kyle said to her. "That clown costume's really cool."

Jamie didn't know what to say. She was fearful
the first instant, but the fear soon evolved into a
certain delightful surprise. "Thanks."

"I'm sorry about today," the boy said sincerely.
"I didn't mean it."

She was stunned. "Really?"

She knew it; it *was* the clown suit. It was a
miracle suit.

"Yeah," Kyle admitted, "I was sort of a jerk."
Then, "Hey, you wanna go with us?"

"Sure!"

Jamie joined the kids, Rachel exhaling arduously, trudging along behind. They walked down the sidewalk and up the cobblestone path to the next house. Rachel waited at the sidewalk again as she watched the kids scramble up to the porch. The kid in the flimsy clown outfit, the boy, rang the doorbell. The front door swung open.

"Trick or treat!" Kyle said, holding out his bag, the other children echoing at his sides.

Kelly stood in the doorway before the parade of candy-moochers, and smiled as she grabbed a fistful of candy from a table just within the entrance. She was wearing absolutely nothing save for an oversized t-shirt with bold, black letters on the front reading COPS DO IT BY THE BOOK. From Rachel's point of view, she appeared ludicrous, standing there before children in that attire. At first, Kelly did not see the other girl gazing in.

Then she did.

Their eyes locked for a moment. Rachel noticed something etched across Kelly's face . . . something like an overwhelming shock . . . or . . . guilt.

"Rachel—" she exclaimed.

Then Rachel saw movement behind her. Curious, she advanced across the cobblestones. The moment she drew close enough to behold what it was she was seeing, she halted. At first, she thought she was mistaken. It didn't take too long for her to realize that she wasn't.

It was Brady.

Holy shit.

It *was* Brady; she was simply having one hell of

107

a time believing it. That bastard. He was there, lounging around on the sofa inside, in the livingroom, his shirt unbuttoned, a beer in his hand. The moment he saw her, the moment the realization absorbed through his consciousness, he bolted to his feet. Kelly was going about her own business with the children as if nothing else interesting was happening.

"Rachel!" Brady was yelling. As the trick-or-treaters went their way to the next household, Rachel turned, her face flushed with mixed anger, disappointment and hurt. Brady continued to call out, running for the door. "Rachel, wait a minute . . . give me a chance to explain!"

Frantically, he sprinted past Kelly, who was gazing on in amusement, and caught Rachel at the sidewalk, grasping her forearm desperately.

She could not meet his gaze; instead, she turned from him, her eyes somewhere upon the darkened street. Softly, she replied back. "You don't owe me anything, Brady. No explanations necessary."

Contemptuous, she pulled her arm free, only for Brady to regain his grip. It was even tighter this time, and she winced, trying unsuccessfully to pull away.

"Listen," this bastard was saying, "you blow off our date at the last minute . . ."

"So you hop on the next best thing!" she yelled. "I thought you were different from the other guys."

"I *am* different," he pleaded. "I was just pissed off, that's all."

"Oh, really? Well, I'll just let Little Miss Hot Pants get back to nursing your bruised ego."

Finally, Rachel managed to break free and walk away, leaving Brady standing there, watching her as she went.

"Rachel!"

"Brady," called another voice, a female voice, emanating from the house. It was sensual; beckoning. It was Kelly. "Are you coming?"

Brady looked back at the figure in the doorway. She was standing there, longing for him, silhouetted under the porch light, the outline of her figure visible beneath the thin t-shirt.

****

Rachel half-trotted down the center of the empty street under the few scattered lamp posts. The encounter with Brady had made her lose track of Jamie, and now Jamie and her little band of midgets had vanished. There was absolutely no sign of them anywhere. In fact, there was absolutely no sign of *anyone*, for that matter. It was as if her very presence had summoned all the citizens of the town into their homes.

At first this absence didn't phase her; the bastard *ex*-boyfriend of hers rattled her brains to such an extent that they were like a puzzle that some little kid came across and tore apart, flinging the black and white pieces into the air. In order for her to think soundly again, the pieces had to be regained. Rachel had to face the possibility that some of these pieces may be forever lost, and it was all because of the little kid symbolized as Brady. Yes, her life was black and white; she felt that nobody ever had their life totally together and figured out. But at least she knew the puzzle fit. Now, it may not ever fit again.

She knew she was a typical seventeen-year-old girl. Once, her school counselor had a talk with her about her class schedule—one of the teachers suggested she belonged in a higher English class, and one thing led to another—and it was this counselor who told her that she appeared to understand about herself more than was usual for someone her age. She didn't agree with him at first, but later she realized that he might have been right. She had a sort of phobia that she kept to herself; a phobia about presenting herself as being too egotistical, talking about herself too much, and so whenever she saw a problem in a friend she thought she could help, she would most likely say nothing. Of course, there were exceptions, but she didn't want to be a "miss know-it-all." Who knows, maybe she'd be a counselor herself when she got older.

But this was all complicated, an overwhelming, often unbearable botchery of living, and explaining the whole thing proved to be even more frustrating and confusing. All she could think of was the puzzle. The missing pieces. And . . .

Brady.

But she'd rather not think about him. That bastard. He was such a typical guy, and she had him figured out to be something else. Perhaps her coun-selor *was* wrong. Maybe she was just lucky when it came to understanding people. Then again, she wasn't perfect.

I mustn't dwell on this, she told herself. *I must not let something like this get me on. I have to show him that I'm not jealous anymore; that I could just as easily drop him and go on to some-one else and not think twice about it. I must.*

She realized she was dwelling on the subject too much. She had to concentrate on her current prob-lem: *she had lost Jamie.*

Well, not *lost*. Wasn't that putting things a bit drastically? Actually, though, there was no other word she could think of to replace it. Yes, Jamie was lost. Jamie was . . .

"Jamie?" she called.

There was nothing. Not a sound around her save for the rustling of maple leaves around her feet and down the street and sidewalks; the gentle swaying of the trees in the wind, the shutters at the win-dows of nearby houses to the left and to the right.

"Jamie?" she spoke louder.

Still, there was no sign of life in the streets.

"Just great," Rachel grumbled to herself. "Just wonderful, Rach. First you lose your boyfriend, then you lose your sister."

She could not seem to be able to get over the fact that there was *absolutely no one around*, where once there were dozens of clusters of trick-or-treaters and opened screen doors. True, the porch lights of many of the houses were still on, but . . .

was Halloween over with? She checked her watch.

Suddenly she thought she heard something; something almost behind her and to her right. She recognized it as a sort of a loud, echoing crackling sound, like that of a . . . a . . . what did it sound like? A twig. It was the sound of a twig snapping amidst the rustling of the leaves. She turned toward the sound.

There, a half of a block away, hovering in the darkness beneath the phantom-like blackness of a tree alongside a parked car, was a face. It was a white face, suspended there, and as close as Rachel dared squint her eyes to see, she could not visually detect the presence of a connecting body. The shadowy-white face just hung; no, *floated*, there, like the cabalistic configuration of a mime wearing nothing but black save for a painted on face. But this face did not seem to possess any specific features; of course, she was too far from the figure to tell, but it appeared as if whatever it was she was gazing at had no eyes.

But this glimpse was momentary, and within the next second the whiteness was gone, having suddenly withdrawn into the obscurity of the night.

She stood there, profoundly startled, looking fearfully into the space where the thing—whatever it was—had been, or she *thought* it had been. It didn't take her very long at all to realize that the streets were empty . . . *so totally empty* . . . and she was a girl alone in the center of a lonely street.

Slowly, she drew in a breath and managed to

call out, attempting to show no signs of fear. "Who's there?"

But there was only the forlorn answer of the wind rustling against hedges, stirring the leaves.

Her frustration with the recent past had now switched dramatically to fear of the present. Nonetheless, she knew she had to find Jamie, had to find *anybody*, even if it was Brady, just to feel safe again. She advanced a step, then her pace quickened down the street once more until the dark figure appeared abruptly in front of her.

She halted.

She could see now that there *was* a body attached to it, a body of extensive proportion, a man's body, and she could see that he was garbed in ragged mechanic's coveralls that appeared not to fit him properly. He remained there, at the end of the block, a tall, unmoving figure, standing as if engaged with Rachel in an old-fashioned showdown she'd seen in the old Westerns on tv. But, unlike those old Westerns, she felt an overwhelming surge of terror and panic. For another lingering moment, neither Rachel nor the shadow figure moved. They simply stood there, eyes staring into hollow eyes.

Then Rachel ran.

She darted to her left, hurrying across a nearby lawn like a frightened animal, vanishing between two dark houses. It was only after she leaped over an old wooden fence, ran through a back yard, and into the next street when she finally managed to conjure up an urgent cry. It was then when she realized there were a few lingering groups of trick-or-treaters still making their rounds from house to house, and she knew she was somewhat safe.

"Jamie!"

She called out the name of her foster sister, this time in desperation, and she slowed in her running as a few children turned their masked heads in effort to see what the commotion was about. Regaining her breath, Rachel managed another anguished cry.

Chapter Thirteen

A precipitant crash generated from within the Caruthers' home, and the sounds echoed to all hallways and rooms, lightly vibrating windows and the glass chandelier situated over the dining table, the room adjacent to the kitchen.

The front door had smashed completely in, splintering partially and knocking a painting of clowns laughing on a beach from the wall. Carefully, cautiously, letting his twelve gauge lead the way, Sheriff Meeker entered. Behind him, stepping into the livingroom with equal circumspection, was Doctor Loomis, his 9mm Smith and Wesson in his hand and ready.

Meeker had been a deputy in those cold, horrific days when death had walked into the quiet streets. And at the time, the entire police force knew how to handle this Michael Myers fellow. It was very simple: *kill him. Shoot the bastard down.* But, after all this time, the very thought of merely shooting the bastard down seemed all too easy. Vaguely, this was like a dream to the sheriff. A hazy, obscure sort of dream at that, and he feared that somewhere within the confines of the next few minutes, this obscure dream would detour into the terror of nightmare.

Regardless, Meeker knew no matter how hauntingly miraculous the circumstances were, or at least seemed to be, Michael Myers was . . . well, stoppable. To Meeker, the good Doctor Loomis was a desperate, complicated man who had been through hell, and that very same hell was what this damn doctor was somewhat responsible for. Sure, the government stuck their asses in the situation somewhere, but the doctor could have done something, could have fought the orders to first transfer this ungodly murderer ten years back. He could have taken the matter to court . . . could have . . . hell, could have done *some goddamn thing*. On the other hand, he had suddenly developed somewhat of a sense of trust for Loomis. And this trust was built upon the fact that nobody knew this monster better than he. Good ol' Doctor Loomis. Good ol' Goddamn Doctor Loomis.

But Meeker knew what he was doing, too. If this *was* true, if Myers *had* somehow escaped captivity and returned to Haddonfield, the sheriff was sure as all hell that he was not about to let a repeat of ten years ago unfold this night. He grew up in this cozy Illinois town, and he was not about to let it go into oblivion at the hands of a psycho.

But this man was more than a psycho. He recalled how Loomis had informed him dozens of times that *he's not a mere psychopath. You must understand . . . he is unadulterated evil.*

But, the sheriff thought to himself, *soon ˌnough, he's gonna be unadulterated dog shit. T ˌat is to say, if he's actually here.*

****

Loomis felt for the wall-mounted light switch in the darkened room and flooded the room with light. It was a little girl's bedroom, complete with dolls, an over abundance of them, and brightly colored little girl's toys and a dresser and bedsheets and . . . he noticed the window was open, the wind blowing eerily through the pink curtains. He went over to it, inspected the area outside momentarily, then shut the window and disassociated himself from the cold. He turned, and his attention diverted toward the opened closet. As he held his gun directly before him, he gently used his feet in moving the doors of the closet further open. When he was quite sure all was definitely clear, he eased his way inside for further inspection. There was a scattering of photographs at his feet, and he bent down to examine them. There appeared to be at least a dozen of them. It did not surprise him in the least when he met with the familiarities of Laurie Strode . . . her husband . . . and there, there was their little daughter. Their little girl, Jamie Lloyd. So innocent.

His gaze met yet another familiarity, and the mere sight seemed to stiffen his sense momentarily. There, to his left, was the photograph of Michael and Judith Myers.

A shuffling to his side—it was Meeker, stepping up to join him. Loomis raised the picture to eye level.

"Something?" Meeker spoke.

"He's been here," Loomis told him plainly. There was a slight tremor in his voice.

Meeker stepped in closer, his eyes focusing on whatever it was Loomis held. "How do you know?"

And with that, the doctor stood aside, disclosing yet another discovery—

The mangled heap of the labrador.

It was Meeker's turn to experience the coldness that the doctor felt.

Meeker spoke, "This thing's starting to spook me, Doc."

"At least I'm not alone."

"Oh?" the sheriff said, being unable to bring himself to believe the doctor could, with his experience, be exactly balls to the wall with fear. "How long have *you* been scared?"

"Twenty-five years."

Loomis had seen enough. He turned and moved past Meeker towards the door, and the sheriff followed him out, finding his gaze difficult to remove from the remains of what had once been the family pet.

Downstairs in the livingroom, the two met a deputy waiting for them near the entrance. As

Meeker allowed Loomis to exit the front door, he turned to the deputy, who stood awaiting his command.

"Logan," Meeker ordered, "I want you here just in case the family comes home."

"Right here, Ben," Logan replied.

"Look sharp. Understand?"

Immediately, the deputy double-checked the chambered rounds in his .38 long barrel. "No problem, Sheriff."

As Meeker closed the front door, he secretly wished the man luck; he had an idea what the town would be up against, but a mere idea wasn't enough.

And this was going to be one hell of a night.

Chapter Fourteen

The smoke filled pool hall and bar lounge was filled to capacity with the town's usual beer bellied personalities, sucking down beers and shooting eight balls in exchange for a chance of good luck at earning a little sum of money. It was a typical setting for a town such as Haddonfield, where everyone knew how many teeth everyone else had or didn't have and didn't really give a shit either way. Friends were friends, and enemies were enemies, and the only enemies in Haddonfield were the out-of-town truck driving brawlers who came into Haddonfield to pick fights, and the winter weather. But now, at this time, they had neither. There were no strangers tonight. Well, perhaps there were a few, but they remained virtually unnoticed amid the bar noise and the laughter. There was a woman in skimpy clothes who always had a fancy for the jukebox, which was at the time blurting out Bruce Springsteen. As the Boss sang about dancing in darkness, she attracted the attentions of a young, mustachioed man who offered to buy her a beer and called her Charlene. Across the way, a middle-sized man in overalls knocked over his half-full bottle of beer onto the pool table. He pulled a flimsy handkerchief from a pocket and frantically wiped away the liquid before it could be completely absorbed by the blue-green felt padding.

Earl Ford was the bartender. His son, Mel, had recently turned legal age and now assisted him, and occasionally there was Hughy who helped him on busy nights like this, but tonight Hughy was sick with the stomach flu. This was Earl's joint, and that was what the tattered baseball bat read in bold, black lettering up above the half-sized swordfish on the wall behind him. Earl was pretty close to forty-five, but his true age was somewhat of a mystery because he always liked folks to keep guessing. It was a belief among some that ol' Earl never really knew his own age, or that he somehow forgot. His face was like that of a bulldog, and he had the body of a professional wrestler, but he, in fact, despised wrestling with a passion. He would often tell people he didn't quite rightly know why he hated it so, but perhaps it was the fact that the matches were so damn fake. Besides, wrestlers looked like a bunch of fags out there on the mat, and the audience looked like a bunch of drunken Nazis. At least, that's what he thought.

Tonight was an ordinary night, or at least it had been, until something caught Earl's attention on the television. He was often distracted by the 22-inch television, always watching for Ernest commercials or commercials with Joe Isuzu, but this time what attracted his attention was something quite different. He stepped over to the set and raised the volume. A news anchorwoman was explaining something which seemed to be urgent. Hell, *of course* it was urgent; anything that said SPECIAL BULLETIN in the background was unusual and urgent. And from what Earl's ears picked up, it sounded like the woman was talking about evacuating the streets.

What the hell?

"By order of the Sheriff's office," the anchorwoman continued, "all citizens of Haddonfield are asked to clear the streets."

Still, the bartender could not hear. *Goddammit.*

"Everybody shut up a goddamn minute!" he yelled out, and the bar quieted, heads turning. Still, some people just could not hear straight. "I said, goddammit, everyone shut up!"

Silence. The anchorwoman continued.

". . . remain indoors until further notice. All businesses are asked to close as soon as possible. Stay tuned to the station for updates."

A tall man, Orrin Wesley, called out, "What's all that shit, Earl?"

That was exactly what Earl was about to ask Meeker himself, or whoever the hell was at the office. Immediately, he moved to the bar's wall mounted phone. He picked up the receiver and dialed hurriedly.

"Who you callin'?" another man asked.

Earl replied, "Police station. I ain't closing down without a good goddamn reason."

Everyone waited. All eyes in the bar rested on Earl. In the background, a few men continued to quietly resume a game of pool, ears open. After a few lingering moments, Earl angrily hung up the phone. He proceeded to remove his bar smock.

"Well?" Orrin asked.

"It just rang," was all Earl would reply.

Within the next minute the entire place was ringing with the sounds of chairs moving and shoes brushing against the wooden floor. Voices of curiosity added to the commotion as the crowd proceeded to follow the bartender out into the front of the bar, through the single front door, past the DON'T DRINK AND DRIVE sign, and out onto the asphalt of the car crammed parking lot.

Yet another follower rushed up to the bartender from within the crowd; asking where the hell he was going and why the hell everyone was following him, knowing full well he was just as dumbfounded as everyone else about the sudden urgency of the news report.

"We're goin' to see Ben," Earl told him angrily. "Phone never just rings at a police station. No way, no how."

Everyone piled into their respective vehicles—pickups, four-wheel drive Blazers, Jeeps, Broncos, and the like, all covered with enough dirt to pave a small street. Earl's Chevy was the first to kick up a wave of dust, and he led the way as the other filled the street from behind.

One hell of a night, all right.

Chapter Fifteen

Guests exited Justin Fallbrook's palatial home, all dressed in their finest attire, some half drunk, others having had little or nothing to drink, but all having enjoyed the party. They were walking to the rows of cars parked along the side of the street, wondering what the urgency was in the news flash. Some had attempted to call the police station, but got no answer. Still, they would comply with the warning, and perhaps call the station later from their own homes.

Richard and Darlene Caruthers stepped across the walkway down the front lawn; one of the couples who had apparently very little to drink.

"Let's drive home first," Darlene said. "Rachel said they wouldn't be out long."

Richard looked around and spotted who he was looking for. "There's Justin. I better say goodnight."

"Richard—" Darlene called after him, but

he was already on his way to speak to the man.

He called out to his wife behind him, "I'll take two seconds."

He went over to Justin Fallbrook, a man in his late forties, and a very wealthy man at that. He was in the process of bidding an older couple goodnight.

"Justin," Richard spoke out to him.

Mr. Fallbrook turned. In a kindly but nonetheless worrisome voice, he said to him, "Richard, I'm so sorry you can't stay for dinner."

"I hope you understand," Richard said.

"No apologies," he replied. "Children come first in my book, too. Look. I'll see you tomorrow morning on the third floor. Nine sharp. Okay?"

Richard was momentarily stunned. With a mixture of delightful surprise, he exclaimed, "Third floor?" At first, he wasn't sure he quite understood, then the reality crept over him and he wholeheartedly welcomed it. "I got it?" He felt like a little kid.

Behind him, Darlene was calling him. "Richard, come on."

Richard was overcome with both relief and tremendous joy. This was something that he had worked very, very hard for. Very hard indeed. "I got it!" he cried.

Darlene came up behind him and clenched his arm. The door to their car was opened, and it didn't take too long for the two to make it inside and drive away, their car intermingled with the moderate flow of traffic the news report had created from the Fallbrook party.

All the way home, Richard kept repeating, "This was one hell of an evening, let me tell you."

Chapter Sixteen

An open lot dotted with the lofty, darkened configurations of towers marked the presence of the Haddonfield Transformer Station. A network of city power cables sprawled out into the night in all directions like hundreds of giant, many-legged spiders in their blackened webs.

A utility truck was parked beside a main circuit junction box, and nearby there was a lone utility worker carrying out routine maintenance on opened power panels. As he wearily continued to work, taking an obscure sort of electrical tool and placing it into the trail of brightness flooding from his pocket flashlight, he brought his gloved fingers around multitudinous wires and switches and carefully went about his adjustments. He paused for a brief moment and removed from his pocket a package of Wrigley's, opened the wrapper, and popped a stick between his teeth.

Suddenly he looked up.

There, not far from his truck, stood the darkened shape of a man. It began to move, taking a few dilatory steps across the expanse of the lot, passing close by in shadow.

"Hey," the worker shouted. "Hey, shit-for-brains! This is city property. No trespassing."

The shape continued to walk. Frustrated and angry, the worker moved away from the junction box and stepped into the shape's path. The shape continued toward him until the man reached out his hand, planting it firmly on the figure's chest and stopping him cold.

"Are you *deaf*? Or are you just stupid?" Absolutely nothing from the shape. It stood motionless, facing the worker. "I could have you arrested, asshole." Still, there was no response. The worker could hear the breathing sounding in slow, hissing emmissions from behind whatever the hell this man was wearing over his face—something like a large, distorted white mask. The worker continued with the Halloween freak.

"You are one dumb son of a bitch," he exclaimed, finally. The thing before him was giving him the chills; this was way too strange, and here he was, out there, alone amidst the low humming of the power cables. "All right, I'm on the radio to the police right now. Don't even think about leaving."

The worker went back toward his truck. Behind him, the shape proceeded to follow. The worker quickly spun around, startled at the shape's sudden proximity.

Silence. No one made the slightest movement. Until . . .

A hand shot out from the obscurity of the shape and clenched the man's neck. Stunned, there was little time for the worker to struggle. He managed a swift kick, then another—both legs flinging into open air at the thing's side. In his overwhelming terror, he realized that he was no longer on the ground. He was being held there, fighting helplessly for his life, and it was then, at that very moment, that he knew he was going to die. He could feel the coldness of the shape's hand, feel the sensation of it seeping through his skin as if his neck were made from a gelatinous putty. He attempted a scream, but the wind inside of him found no means for escape. He feared that at any time his neck would simply snap from the force.

Then the shape lifted him even further from the ground and flung his limp body into the circuit junction box, impaling him. Amidst his own blood and flesh sizzling against the flying spark he finally managed a single, agonizing scream.

Then it was all over.

His dead body remained quivering there as the shape watched, its head cocked in morbid fascination. The box continued to short circuit around the body, and all around the encompassing area the transformers began to shower a spectacle of sparks. Lightning arcs of rampant power surges began to shatter cables. The station's transformers began to turn into a forest of flaming brilliance, storms of electricity errupting from all directions.

The shape continued to walk on. The last of his presence developed into a silhouette against the festivity of powerful light, then it disappeared in the direction of the town and into the night.

In the streets of Haddonfield, true and ultimate darkness set in.

Chapter Seventeen

Throughout the entire town, darkness set in as the electrical power died. Parents rushed their children into cars. Others pulled their kids from the sidewalk and behind closed doors, a sense of undefined panic clouded their faces.

Panic indeed. It ran rampant through Haddonfield this Halloween night. Panic of not knowing what was going on, panic spawned by what the news people were saying on their television sets intermingled with the sudden power failure. Some didn't take the mysterious circumstances all too seriously, thinking that the whole thing would all blow over shortly and that the town would be up again on its feet. But there were the others, terrified, not knowing what to do except to heed the final words of the news report and to stick close together with their families behind locked doors, huddled close to burning candles and emergency kerosene lamps.

Jamie wandered through the darkened streets as

the last remaining children were scurried into cars and driven off, including the small band that she had joined. Kyle had been suddenly picked up by his mother, who had scolded him for failing to come when she called him over the first time.

Now, she was left alone.

She didn't understand what what going on. All she knew was that all the lights in all the houses and all the street lamps around her had died, and right before that parents had shown up, grabbing their kids in a frantic rush and taking them home. Something was certainly *wrong* here, and Jamie was certainly scared. She looked around for Rachel, but her foster sister was no where to be found.

"Rachel?" she cried out once, and once was enough. Her own voice frightened her, perhaps because its echoes made her realize how alone she was in the darkened street.

Now, there was only wind and silence. She turned and began to cross the deserted street eyes darting this way and that, searching for any sign of Rachel . . . or even *somebody* . . . as long as it wasn't . . . the nightmare man.

No; please, no. She didn't want to think about that. Not now, not ever. But there, in the darkness, when everyone suddenly deserts you, a little girl's thoughts could run wild.

She'd dare not think of him. She'd dare not think of how she stepped into her uncle at the Discount Mart, how he scared her, how he reached out.

Then it hit her. *Maybe that was why everyone suddenly went away. Maybe it was because the nightmare man was coming.*

No, Jamie. Don't think about it. Don't *even*. You're just getting yourself even more scared than ever.

She was shivering. She realized she had to look for Rachel, and that Rachel was probably looking for her, too.

Please, God. Don't let anything happen to Rachel. Please.

Jamie didn't know that what she was fearing all along was just behind her, a little way into the darkness along the street's opposite side, tracking her, watching her every move through the hollow of its mask. Finally, it appeared almost directly behind her, stepping out into the middle of the lane.

Jamie reached another corner and stopped. The sound of another pair of footsteps continued for another second longer from her rear, then stopped as well. Quickly, the little girl spun around towards the sound.

There was nothing but emptiness.

"Rachel?" she called out, her voice cracking. "Is that you?"

Still, there was nothing. No answer.

She turned and proceeded along the vacant street, the eeriness of her haunting surroundings growing, aching throughout her mind and tugging on her nerves.

Stopping in her tracks once more, the second

137

echoing steps continued. They were closer now. Then they halted.

The little girl turned again.

In a firm but innocent voice, shaking, she told the darkness, "Whoever you are, I've got a big dog with me. He bites."

But again there was no reply.

She stood still, waiting to hear something, anything, but all there appeared to be was the encompassing darkness. As she stood there, she heard the footsteps once again. They were approaching her, and she could not see a single soul. Her eyes searched frantically.

"You hear me, I've got a dog," she managed to speak out, but it only sounded forth in a mere whisper.

She tried to run this time, but she found that she couldn't. She was frozen in place, stiff, like a terrified rabbit knowing that there was a python in its cage ready to feed but not knowing where it was.

The footsteps were growing closer . . .

. . . closer still . . .

. . . until . . . suddenly . . .

She miraculously began to run. Her movements were fast and swift, the wind on her back helping her along. In the midst of her panic, she nearly fell. She was paying more attention to what was behind her than where she was going, panting and gasping tremendously, barely being able to breathe. She almost swore she was going to simply die from exhaustion before whoever it was that followed could get to her. The world before her now was a whirlwind, bucking and yawing in one fantastic fit of frenzy. Then she ran directly into a figure, nearly knocking it down and her along with it. She uttered a startled scream as hands grabbed at her, and she fought them blindly. It was no use. The hands caught hold.

Rachel bent down close to her.

"Jamie," Rachel said, fearfully, "Jamie, calm down. Jamie, where have you been?" After both girls caught their breath, Rachel having been running herself, she scolded her. "Don't *ever* run off on your own at night. You hear me? Not *ever*!"

Suddenly the two girls were washed in the brightness of automobile headlights. A car swerved to the curb and stopped, and within the next second, Sheriff Meeker and Doctor Loomis began to climb out and rush over to them. Meeker was the first to cry out.

"Rachel Caruthers. Jamie Lloyd. Thank God."

The two girls were confused. But that was only part of it.

"What's going on?" Rachel demanded.

The other man with the overcoat spoke out, "Get in the car."

As the two girls reluctantly obeyed, Loomis turned and stopped cold in his tracks.

There in the distance, as far as the darkness could allow him to see and with the assistance of the car's high beams, was Michael Myers. He was simply standing there, motionless, on the sidewalk across the street.

Stricken with fear, Loomis stood frozen. Meeker caught what was happening and followed the doctor's line of sight. Then he saw him.

"Is that him?"

Loomis continued his seemingly thoughtless gaze.

Meeker repeated, desperate, *"Doc, is it him?"*

Loomis quickly and urgently drew out his pistol. *"Yes!"*

Meeker went immediately for his shotgun. Just as he was about to aim, he noticed something— something to his right on his side of the street, a figure standing below the dark branches of a tree.

There, right before his unbelieving eyes, was a second Michael Myers.

Holy shit.

Just then, another Myers—a *third* one, appeared from out of the dark and between the shadows of two houses.

"What," Meeker exclaimed, then the presence of a fourth Myers materialized from behind a Volkswagon.

A fifth.

A sixth.

There was a whole goddamn army of them!

This wasn't a dream anymore, Meeker told himself, inside his mind. *This was a nightmare. One shitload of a nightmare.* And he knew just like the next person did that this sort of thing just didn't happen in real life.

Loomis was equally terrified. Perhaps more so. "Dear God. No. NOOOO!"

Loomis brought up his pistol and aimed at the

140

first one. Just as he was about to fire, the sheriff realized something and knocked the doctor aside, Loomis pulling the trigger. The bullet went into empty air.

Then there was the voice of a child crying out. Before them, across the street, the first Myers took off his mask and revealed the panic stricken face of a tall sixteen-year-old baring freckles and long red hair. He darted into the shadows and disappeared. So did the rest. The kid between the house yelled out something which sounded like *don't shoot!* and he scurried off in kind.

Shouting angrily, Meeker ordered them all out of there. "Get home, goddamn it. There's a curfew. I catch your asses and it's a weekend in jail!"

He turned, and saw Loomis leaning heavily against the squad car. He was trembling, exhaling terribly.

"You okay?" the sheriff questioned him.

"Good God," Loomis managed. "I could've killed a child. What *does* that make me?"

Meeker said, "Let's get back to the station. Get these kids here safe."

But as the squad car swerved away, not one noticed the dark presence behind them, back on the street, its reflection glimmering in the car's rearview mirror until, a heartbeat later, it was gone.

Chapter Eighteen

Headlights swept over the face of the darkened police station and revealed something neither Loomis nor Meeker expected to see. The entire outer portion was in shambles. Meeker had to skid to avoid the shards of broken glass from the doors. Broken fixtures swung in the constant draft in the doorways.

The squad car idled, and Meeker and Loomis crawled out, Meeker charging the two kids to remain in the back seat.

Meeker and Loomis entered through the broken glass double doors, their guns ready and a flashlight scanning. The interior was a veritable ruined nightmare. The cold breeze eminating inward from outside was blowing papers everywhere, from the lopsided desks and onto the floor, and from the floor to all corners of the room. The sheriff was about to flip on the light switch when he remembered there was no power. He shown his flashlight in the area ahead of him and proceeded forward, with utter caution, the doctor coming up on the rear.

Meeker could not understand what his men were doing to allow such a catastrophe to take place; couldn't believe that one man could actually do all this. And where the hell *were* his men, anyway?

"They wouldn't have given up without a fight," Meeker said.

Loomis told him, "They didn't know what they were up against."

Glass crunched under their shoes as they continued inward, past broken desks and desk chairs, past broken telephones and scattered trash. They went around to the side, near a closet door. The flashlight came across a pool of what seemed to be blood from beneath the door. It *was* blood; the sheriff was merely having difficulty believing it. He made the light crawl upwards until it came upon a pale hand, closed in the door jamb. It was clutching a .38 revolver. Reluctantly, Meeker opened the door. There was no body; the hand fell and tumbled, dismembered, splashing into the pool of blood.

"Christ," Meeker exclaimed.

Something caused him to look up, and when he did, he jolted backwards just in time to avoid the pasty white, blood drenched body of Deputy Pierce which leaned out of the darkness near the ceiling, then tumbled to the ground before him in one tremendous splotch. As the body met the ground, the head rolled backwards, revealing dead, unseeing eyes. The throat was slashed, and thick blood seeped from the gaping wound until it rested at the sheriff's feet.

Meeker gazed down in horror upon what was once his best deputy, not to mention one of his best friends. His eyes momentarily refusing to leave the sight, he brought himself to speak. "How can one man do this? How, Loomis? Tell me. How?!"

"He's not a man, Sheriff."

"Then what is he?" Meeker demanded, trembling. *"What the hell are we dealing with?"*

"Evil," Loomis replied, and that was all he said.

Outside, Earl Ford and the other townies were pulling up to the station's parking lot, driving past the library and halting near the sheriff's squad car. Loomis was standing in the doorway, Meeker coming up behind him. Rachel and Jamie gazed on with extreme interest from within the back seat of the squad car.

As the men from the bar stepped out of their respective vehicles, Meeker informed the doctor, quietly, "The other two are in the back . . . dead."

"Ben?" Earl marched up to them. "What the samhill is goin' on?"

A second man by the name of Sam Unger went towards the shattered glass doors and peered inside. "Holy shit. What the hell did this? Terrorists?"

"Go home, Earl," Meeker told him; told them all, in fact, weariness in his voice intermingled with a hard stern overtone. ". . . this is police business."

Earl said, almost sarcastically, "Looks to me like you're *outta* business. I want some answers."

"I don't have the time or the patience to argue with you," the sheriff said, stepping forward past Loomis. "Just go home to your families. That's where you belong."

"You forget who's paying your salary, Sheriff?" That came from Sam Unger.

"It was Michael Myers," Loomis said, and he caught their undivided attention. Meeker shot the doctor an angry glance. "He's come home to kill."

"Oh, Jesus," Earl exclaimed softly, shocked suddenly into a perpetual fear. *"Michael Myers?"*

Meeker interrupted, agitated. "Leave it alone, Earl. Let the police handle it."

But Earl was determined, and he yelled back to the sheriff, emotionally stricken with remembrances of a time gone by. That terrible time, ten years back.

"Let the *police* handle it? Like the last time? How many dead back then? How many kids? Al here, he lost his boy ten year back. Not this time, Ben. I'll handle this my own way." The husky bartender turned to the others, "We're gonna fry his ass. Get your weapons, boys!"

The other townies, grumbling to themselves of the vengeance they would bestow upon the grisly murderer this evening, this old, old evil that had once again returned, followed Earl back to their vehicles. Their Broncos and their Fords and their pickups revved and whirled, swirling and skidding until they reached the street and disappeared past the library.

As soon as they had left, Meeker spun around and faced Loomis angrily. "You stupid son of a bitch! You've just created a lynch mob."

"Without a police force," Loomis said, taking a handkerchief from his coat pocket and wiping the baldness of his head, sweat dribbling down the sides of his face, "those men may be Haddonfield's only defense."

Meeker stepped back and shone his light once again into the ruined shambles of the building. He flicked the switch off and turning, the sheriff knew that he had enough guessing and enough shocking episodes of death. He was going to get to the bottom of this and kill that son of a bitch Myers once and all, and he'd be damned if he didn't get all the help he was going to need.

"Then God help us," he replied to Loomis.

As they started back to the squad car, Loomis said, "We still need a place for the child."

"My house," Meeker said immediately. "It's secure, and I've got a shortwave in the basement. We can call the State Police."

As they climbed into the squad car, leaving the Sheriff's station nightmare behind for the time being, they disappeared into the darkness of the silent streets. It was then the sheriff realized that hell was too goddamn moderate for describing what the remainder of the night would be like.

Chapter Nineteen

The front door to the Caruthers' house swung open and Logan exited, hurryingly closing it behind him and not bothering to check the lock. His mind was on the urgency at hand, and this was no time for trivialities. He rushed from the house to the squad car, climbed into the driver's side and started the engine. He snatched up the car's police radio.

"Ben, I'm on my way," he reported into it. Then, he added, "Were they really—?"

"I know how you feel," Meeker's voice came in. "Just get over to my house right away."

"Be there in five minutes."

As he pulled out of the driveway, he thought he saw something in the rear view mirror. He turned, seeing only darkness.

But as he traveled down the street, the black figure remained within the shadows of the back seat.

Motionless.

Waiting.

Chapter Twenty

Candles glowed and flickered with a subtle resplendence atop the television set and the fireplace mantel, providing a maudlin atmosphere for the two lovers embracing, stretched across the carpet below. They were lying there together, alone, and their kisses grew long and passionate as time vanished into a vague simplistic notion called the past; they were entranced inside the sheer delicacy of their intermingled world.

Kelly leaned up from the carpet and gazed down dreamily upon Brady beneath her. Her long t-shirt draped downwards and spread across the faded logo of his own shirt. Brady's hands moved underneath and up along the smoothness of her skin.

Kelly spoke softly, "Let's go upstairs."

"I don't want to wait," Brady whispered in reply.

The girl was thoroughly delighted with livingrooms as much as bedrooms or *anywhere* for that matter.

She smiled down upon him teasingly. Slowly, she slipped off her t-shirt, pulling it over her head and dropping it to one side. Her eyes were saturated into his, watching with playful curiosity the somber yet hungry expressions his face displayed. She reached behind her and unsnapped her bra. She allowed it to slide to the carpet. Her panties were of lace, and as Brady's eyes glided across her body and downwards, he could see the triangle of pubic hair daintily exhibited before him.

"What do you think?" she breathed.

Brady let out a sigh of ecstacy. "I think I'm in heaven."

He reached and pulled Kelly on top of him, and as they kissed he writhed out of his shirt and flung it over the coffee table nearby. Kelly worked her lips erotically down across the surface of his chest, her hands skimming past his sides and to his waist. Her fingers played with the buckle of his pants until it separated, and she drove her soft hands into his underwear, searching and grasping, sliding his pants down to his knees. His skin rippled with desire. He brought her down to him once again, and as tongues caressed he held her, his hands moving down the backside of her voluptuous body, finding her panties and bringing them down to her legs. She kicked them off of her feet.

The two fondled and caressed each other within the sensuality of the semi-darkness. As the minutes ticked by and the quickened heat increased, Kelly wrapped her legs around his, welcomingly, and he moved his body upwards to enter her.

"Oooh, Brady," she moaned.

"Oh, *shit!*"

Headlights flooded the livingroom mingled with the whining sounds of a car engine. Brady sat up in terror. Kelly joined him, sitting up also. Immediately, her hands went for her clothes and she proceeded hurryingly to get dressed.

"It's my dad," she muttered. "If he catches us like this he'll skin you alive for starters."

"For starters?" Brady panicked, reaching for his clothes in a frenzy. "Christ. Oh, man."

Nothing seemed to fit right for him, and he nearly put his pants on backwards. God knew his underwear didn't feel right, and he thought he heard the ripping of its pliant fabric.

Outside, Sheriff Meeker brought out his house keys, fussed for one, and inserted it into the doorknob. Behind him, Rachel and Jamie stepped up to the porch followed in turn by Doctor Loomis.

"Where's the deputy?" Loomis questioned, anxious.

Meeker answered him as the door opened, "He'll be here in a minute."

Just as the deputy's presence was mentioned, Logan's squad car approached, highbeams piercing through the darkness of the driveway with near blinding brilliance. It pulled up and halted, Logan stepping out onto the cement.

Meeker turned and entered his home, all others following in turn.

As he stepped across the foyer and into the livingroom, his eyes beheld his daughter and the boy. Their gazes met but for a moment, the two standing dead center near the fireplace and the television amidst the moderate blaze of the candles, their appearance was as if they had just completed a night's rest but their faces were sweaty with guilt.

The burly sheriff's gaze shot past them as if they did not exist.

My God, he's ignoring us, Brady told himself, trembling. *Holy shit, he's gonna act like we're not here, and then he's gonna let me have it. That's it. Let me have it when I least expect it, and then there won't be anything left of me to send back home.*

Meeker's urgency and alertness confused the boy momentarily, until it suddenly struck him that the sheriff had more important matters at hand; he remembered what the announcer had said on television.

Then he saw Rachel, and their eyes met. Quickly, and with utter embarrassment, he turned away.

"Rachel," Meeker promptly ordered, "take your sister upstairs. Last door at the end of the hall."

Rachel nodded and took Jamie upstairs.

Her mind swirling amidst the abrupt confusion, Kelly went to her father. "Dad, what's going on?"

He turned to her, eyes serious and demanding. "I want you to secure all the downstairs windows. Cover all the downstairs windows."

"Why?"

"Just do it!"

Without further hesitation, Kelly complied.

"Where's the radio?" Loomis said.

"Through the kitchen to the basement door," Meeker directed. "Take my flashlight."

Loomis reached and took the flashlight Meeker held, turned, and exited out the kitchen in a hurry, nearly knocking over Meeker's daughter as she went about her business.

Now for the boy.

Meeker turned and grabbed him, clenching his arm firmly. Brady broke out in nervous perspiration, knowing he was about to get hurt. Instead . . .

"You know how to handle a gun?" Meeker said.

What?

Meeker repeated himself. "A gun. Know how to use one?"

"Yes, sir." His voice shook.

At the same time, Logan entered through the front door and joined them, standing, awaiting the sheriff's next orders. Meeker took the boy over to a closet door down the hallway near a back storage room. He opened the door, revealing racks of various shot guns. He let go of the boy and reached inside, immediately gripping a double barrel. He handed it to Brady.

"Think you can handle that?"

"Easy enough," Brady said, confused. "You want to tell me what's happening?"

"When I have time." Then, to Logan, who was stepping up to their right, "Where's your riotgun?"

"In the trunk of my squad," was the reply.

"Get it."

Logan turned on his heels and exited quickly back down the hallway. Meeker returned his gaze to the innards of the closet, reached in once again, this time removing a tool box and handing it to Brady also.

"There's shells for that shotgun in there," he explained. "You also got a hammer an' four boxes a roofing nails. I want you to go up in the attic and secure it so nobody can get in."

Brady wasn't about to panic. But the urgency was there and he could not deny that. "If something's happened I should call my parents—"

"You just get up in that attic," Meeker commanded. Once again he went into the closet, and this time he pulled out an SPAS-12 gauge autoloader. This one was for himself. As he loaded shells into the weapon with long practiced ease, he looked back at Brady, who was disappearing down the hall. "Oh yeah. I catch you groping my daughter again, and I'll use that shotgun on you. *Understand?*"

Brady understood and nodded, then fearfully went his way.

Outside, Logan hustled back to the squad. As he went around its side, he noticed the rear door open on the driver's side. Quickly, he looked in and saw nothing. Shrugging, he slammed the door and went over to the trunk. There was a riotgun inside the trunk, and he removed it along with two large boxes of shells. This was all he needed. Carrying them under one arm he slammed the trunk down

156

hard, and he hurried back into the house, closing the front door behind him.

Inside, on the first floor of the house, Meeker assisted his daughter in locking and securing the shutters and windows. Kelly's nervousness was altogether gone, having been replaced by the present's urgency, although deep inside she regretted the sudden intrusion on a salacious evening. She could sense her father's hardened glances, but when she would glance back she saw him exigently tending to his business.

Logan stepped up to the sheriff, riotgun in hand. Meeker turned to meet him.

"Get the outside shutters," he instructed.

Logan appeared both dazed and alert at the same time. "What are we doing?"

"Making sure nobody can get in here."

"Isn't all this a little paranoid?"

Meeker's glance was stern. "If you'd seen the station house, you wouldn't even ask."

Logan turned again and moved down the long side hallway of the first floor. As he went, he passed a partially opened doorway, and if he had glanced within, even momentarily, he would have seen the blackened view of the figure standing motionless within the darkness, waiting in the shadows.

Inside the basement, Loomis scanned the flashlight over dusty obstructions and obscurities. The basement was a dark, eerie place made up of workbenches, a couple of broken-down ten-speed bikes, an old freezer, boxes upon boxes of junk and unwanted items. His flashlight brushed into a stringy cobweb, and the doctor tore it away and stepped backwards from it. His beam trailed down to yet another workbench.

There, at the far end, was the radio.

****

Brady passed by a window on the way down the upstairs hallway and peeked out for a second's time. He could see the deputy slamming shutters closed over the windows down stairs. After another brief glimpse into the outside darkness of the streets across the way, he moved away from the window and strode through the hall to the partially opened door at the far end. Slowly, he creaked the door opened further and leaned his head inside.

There, in the shadows on the bed, were Rachel and Jamie. They were sitting there, ever so quietly, Rachel holding her younger sister protectively yet calmly.

"Are you two okay?" Brady asked, breaking the silence.

Rachel didn't bother to turn.

"We've been better," she replied sourly.

"What's going on?"

"Michael Myers."

"Who?"

Rachel then finally looked at him. "Ten years ago, Halloween. He's Jamie's uncle."

"The kids at school were right," Jamie interrupted, and suddenly she began to sob.

Rachel turned her gaze away from Brady and rocked her gently, comforting her, wishing they were someplace else . . . someplace far away. Far away from uncles, far away from Brady.

Far away.

Politely, Brady retreated from the bedroom and quietly shut the door, leaving them in the darkness.

At the other end of the hallway, past the staircase, Brady set down the gun and the toolbox and reached above his head to the ceiling. His fingers fumbled for the handle to the attic door, grasped it and brought the attic staircase down. Kneeling, he opened the toolbox and fished out a flashlight, closed the box once more, then brought everything into his arms and climbed the wood stairs into the dust and the blackness.

****

"That's all the windows, Dad," Kelly proclaimed.

Meeker, his daughter, and Logan stood together near the front door, gazing around, thinking if there was anything left to do; anything they just might have overlooked.

"Okay," the sheriff said. "Logan, I want you here on the front door. Here's the deadbolt key."

"Thanks," he said, not knowing why. He took the key from the sheriff, turned, placed it in the deadbolt, and turned it. The bolt flew home with a dull *clack*.

"We're secure," Meeker said. "I padlocked the

back door. This is the only way in or out of the house.''

After another glance toward the door, he turned and went into the kitchen in the direction of the basement staircase.

Logan surveyed the foyer momentarily, then, turning, accidentally bumped into Kelly. The seriousness had left her eyes, replaced with an enticing glare. She grabbed the riotgun barrel with her left hand and, before the stunned deputy, gently stroked it suggestively.

Logan tugged it from her. "Back off, Kelly. I like my job.''

Playfully, seductively, Kelly stepped closer to him. "Just wondered if it was loaded.''

Kelly brushed past the deputy and moved off, past the livingroom candles and into the long side hallway, disappearing.

Logan scratched his head feverishly, then, turning to the rear of the door, wondered what would happen next, and whispered a prayer for daylight.

Chapter Twenty-one

Haddonfield Park, or the Terry Grounds as it was sometimes called for a reason long forgotten by most, was the blackest part of town at night. This was due to the fact someone had flung bricks at the two light posts situated at both ends, and since that incident a few days ago no one had time to fix them.

The darkness was interrupted by the brightness of the headlights of a pickup truck, and the air became filled with the roar of an engine and the multitudinous voice of townies.

Earl Ford's pickup rounded the corner slowly making its way past the park, high power flashlights shining from the hands of the men at the back, scanning the surrounding area carefully. On the opposite side of the street, their beams came across driveways and trash cans, piles of deadened leaves and the front porches of various shaped houses, some baring the flicker of candles from behind closed drapes within the windows.

The men were armed, some with pistols and others with shot guns, ready for any encounter, grumbling to themselves about catching the son of a bitch who had returned to wreak devastation once again upon this town of theirs.

Suddenly, one of them, the once called Orrin, raised a pointing finger and called out, *"There he is!"*

From the front seat, Earl snatched his Remington twelve gauge pump beside him and immediately bailed out of the truck.

The men hopped from the truck's bed and joined him, Orrin continuing to point out the direction which he referred to. Earl slowly marched toward direction, pumping the shotgun to ready. Orrin came up beside him, leading him further, then stopped in his tracks and rested his finger in the direction of a series of heavy bushes beside a modest colonial house.

"I seen his face!" he half-yelled. "Right there, Earl. Right in those bushes."

The other men readied their rifles and shotguns and pistols, all nervous, all shaking, but all as damn well ready as they could ever be in such a desperate moment. Fingers were tense on triggers. There was a long pause of silence before the bushes began to rattle and rustle, then there was a flash of something pale white which darted across the steady beams of their flashlights and seemed to move toward them.

It was then Earl shouted, "FIRE!"

The air turned thunderous with the intensity of

the pandemonium of shotgun blasts as the men opened fire upon the entire range of the bushes. A deafening firestorm of buckshot grew into a violent crescendo which echoed throughout the expanse of the town, and various front doors in the surrounding area opened, curious and startled heads popping out to view the commotion.

Quickly, the bushes began to disintegrate under the constant blasting, and several seconds passed before the last gun finally emptied completely.

Smoke eddied above the ruined hedges. Leaves and branches were blasted virtually to dust. The entire row of what was once hedges stood naked and bare before the determined lynch mob. Nothing was left untouched; toothpicks and sawdust was what there flashlights now beheld, and as the group of men slowly advanced, their flashlights beheld blood.

Then the pulverized body of a man.

One man cried out in horror, "Shit, Earl, that's Ted Hollister!"

Earl swung around to Orrin. "You told me you saw Myers!"

Orrin backed away, defensive, yelling. "You told us to fire, not me!"

Earl dropped his shotgun and hurled a fist at the man, smacking into his left jaw. Jolted backwards against the grass, Orrin rose to his feet and roadblocked Earl into the nearby dust. As both men began to wrestle, others tried despairingly to pull them apart.

Chapter Twenty-two

The darkness of the attic tended to be a bit haunting for Brady as he finished hammering another window shut. Then again, considering the unnerving circumstances, he had every right to feel scared. He remembered the stories about Michael Myers, and he remembered standing there as the ambulances and paramedics surrounded Laurie Strode's house after the bodies had been found—he was only seven years old at the time, but tonight the images were crystal clear in his mind.

Jamies's uncle.

It was difficult to believe. Yet the whole thing sounded vaguely familiar to him; he was almost certain he heard this about Jamie Lloyd before, but he figured he must not have paid any attention to it. It was like a dream, or, more precisely, like *deja vu*, this sudden news.

And Jamie's uncle was here, somewhere, in this very town.

God only knew how many people have been killed already, somewhere out within the depths of the blackout. He realized it could've been him out there, dead, later to be driven away on a stretcher with dozens of eyes gazing on after him. But he wasn't out there now; he was in there. He was safe.

Then again, for some reason, he didn't *feel* safe. He felt vulnerable.

Yet he had no reason to be. He *was* truly safe here. *Everyone* was truly safe here. They had weapons, and there was Sheriff Meeker and a deputy there to protect them. And he would protect Rachel and Jamie. Oh, and yes, he would protect Kelly too. Mustn't forget about Kelly.

That was another matter. As he moved on to the very last window (there were only three windows in the attic, each side by side towards the front of the house), he remembered a few of the momentous times he had shared with Rachel, and he remembered how each one of those times ended with a slight shove from the girl whenever Brady would try to go too far. Kelly wasn't like that. In fact, with Kelly, he didn't even have to make the first move; it was like he was a magnet to her, and she just came to him. Some people called her a slut at one time, with the suicidal boldness to even do it in front of her father, and the ordeal went on until it ended with rock salt up a boy's ass from Meeker's gun. So when it came to notions about *sluts*, well, let's just say it was all hush hush.

Besides, Kelly was a babe, wasn't she? And

there were definitely a few horny guys out there who'd die just to see what Brady saw tonight.

But Rachel; well, that was a different story.

A final swing of the hammer landed painfully on Brady's thumb. The surge of pain shot up through the throbbing bone, and he let out a sudden yelp.

"Jesus!"

He heard a sound from behind him. Something fell from somewhere on the attic's far side. Startled, nearly forgetting his aching thumb, Brady reached for his flashlight, groping. He could only see a slight portion of what the moonlight allowed him to see, and that darkness of the room encompassed the space where the flashlight was supposed to be. As soon as he found it, it toppled over and rolled away from his grip. Finally, he retrieved it and flicked it on. He began to scan the room.

Silence.

"Who is it?" Brady called.

As far as he could see, the attic was vacant. There was nothing but clutter and stored memorabilia, old picture frames and dusty paintings, archaic sculptures, prescriptive metal objects and a boxfull of what seemed to be dartboards. His flashlight beam then centered on a moose-head rocking, slowing into a halt.

Cautiously, Brady advanced deeper into the room, occasionally glancing back at his shotgun resting propped up against the wall where he finished the windows. The blackness descended behind him and he continued, and his figure was chased by numerous shadows.

Still, he found nothing.

****

Rachel stared blankly out the room's window. She gazed down upon the deserted streets across the way, the only illumination being that of the moonlight. Her eyes had become accustomed to the dark. Her thoughts were on fear, on Brady, on the night.

She realized she was growing to hate Halloween. Everything bad happened on Halloween, and she didn't know why. Come to think of it, the same rang true for *all* holidays. She couldn't understand it. She'd ponder upon it in depth later; for now, all she could do was continue to gaze blankly out this window, the possibility of certain doom for both herself and for her foster sister hanging over her head like a curse.

Yes, she was afraid. Deathly afraid. But she knew she mustn't let Jamie know she was. Rachel was there to protect her foster sister. And the only way to protect your foster sister from the nightmare man was to not have any nightmares yourself.

Right?

Rachel managed to move. She turned slightly to Jamie, whose figure she could see on the bed. She was sitting there motionless, gazing down into the palms of her hands. Rachel stood and crossed over to her, kneeling down beside her.

She spoke in a soft, comforting whisper. "I want you to lie down and try to go to sleep."

"I can't sleep," the little girl responded gazing up at her darkened outline. "The nightmare man will come. He'll get me."

Lovingly, Rachel lay Jamie backwards on the bed and pulled a folded comforter up and over her arms. She had to be delicate, for Jamie was a delicate little six-year-old.

"Nobody's gonna get you while I'm around," Rachel told her. She felt for her sister's hair and gently caressed it.

"Promise?"

"Promise," she replied. "Now close your eyes."

Jamie said, "Can we go home soon, Rachel?"

Rachel thought momentarily, then, "Real soon, kiddo." Another pause. "Real soon. Now, shhhh."

****

The flashlight flickered in Loomis' hands. He firmly tapped it with his palm and it resumed to shine upon the front of the shortwave radio's instruments. He was standing, stooped over the sheriff's shoulders as the sheriff sat before the device, adjusting it as was necessary.

"How is it powered?" Loomis asked him.

"Batteries. I was planning a generator for the house next week. Wish I hadn't waited." After making the proper final adjustments, Meeker drew the radio microphone to his lips. He spoke into it. "This is Squawk seven niner zero Haddonfield broadcasting on State Police emergency frequency. Does anyone hear me?"

The radio hissed in reply.

****

Downstairs, Kelly proceeded to make coffee by candlelight, boiling water in a kettle over a gas flame burner in the kitchen. She possessed only one candle; the remainder were in the livingroom and foyer, giving company to Logan, who'd pulled up an easy chair and sat there with the riotgun in his lap. He seemed to be alert, and whenever Kelly glanced his way she could see that his eyes rarely wandered far from the front door.

As she stood watching him, she remembered the intimacy between herself and Brady that evening. She was stricken with an overwhelming sense of disappointment, but she realized that there was simply nothing she could do at the moment. Besides, her father was there.

Oh well; she had enough to worry about. There was no power, and there was a crazed lunatic killer somewhere out on the streets. Things couldn't really get any worse.

Could they?

The wind outside rustled branches against the window glass, momentarily startling her. She took a second to glance around the empty kitchen. Like most children, she used to be afraid of the dark. She experienced a slight chill and told herself that there was nothing to fear but the dark itself. Or did the saying go *there's nothing to fear but fear itself*? Anyway, it was something like that.

But regardless of how the saying went, regardless of how many excuses she could give herself or how she tried to explain it away, she knew she was afraid.

****

Upstairs, in the master bedroom, Rachel stood and leaned over her foster sister, lightly kissing her forehead.

All was quiet around the two girls, and Jamie was finally dozing under the comforter. Rising, careful not to awaken the sleeping child, she gave her a final glance, after which she silently exited the room, leaving the door ajar.

The hall was nearly a pitch black, and the adjustment Rachel's eyes had developed to the lack of light didn't seem to aid her all that much. As she felt for the side wall, she made her way down the hallway's blackness. She cursed herself for not being equipped with a flashlight. Surely the sheriff himself possessed other flashlights hidden somewhere around the house. She could have asked, but at the time she simply had given no thought about it.

Barely up ahead, she could view the ghostly outline of the top of the staircase. She reached out and grabbed part of the top portion of the banister. Slowly, she began to descend.

Step by careful step, she made her way down to

the bottom end and into the glow of the livingroom candlelight from the fireplace and the television.

There was the deputy, seated in the easy chair, his body facing the front door. As soon as the young lady moved into his line of sight, he spoke to her and she turned.

"Everything okay?"

"Jamie's sleeping," she told him quietly. The dark atmosphere had a certain property which made everyone seem to whisper for no clear reason. Still, however, she didn't mind. What she *did* mind was getting the hell out of this situation. "Jamie's sleeping. When can we go home?"

"State Police'll come," Logan assured her. "Not long after that. Don't worry."

"I'm trying," she said.

Actually, she had plenty to worry about; for the figure that watched from the shadows behind them, the figure that stood there, motionless, that eventually drifted back into the confines of their shared darkness, was waiting, his unearthly mind contemplating patiently behind the pasty white blankness of his mask.

****

Meeker tuned the radio's receiver again for a clear message, and a voice began to fade in. Loomis leaned close to the speaker, listening intently.

"I hear someone," he said.

From the radio came a low, semi-raspy utterance, then the voice came in more lucid. "This is

Frank Butte over in Tuckerville. You got some kind of emergency?''

"Thank Christ," Meeker exclaimed. Then into the microphone, "Yes, this is Ben Meeker, the sheriff over in Haddonfield. Our power and phone lines are down and we've got a killer loose in our streets. Michael Myers.''

The voice sounded perplexed and angered. "This some kind a Halloween prank?''

Meeker's voice was tense. "This isn't a joke. We need the State Police and we need them *now*!''

A pause. "I'll give 'em a call right away. Hang on a sec, I'm gonna need name and address.''

"We're not going anywhere, Mr. Butte.''

Loomis exhaled, relieved. At least, he was somewhat relieved. Now these people would be safe. The State Police would be there soon. Now, he knew what he personally had to do. He turned and proceeded to climb the stairs to the kitchen.

Inside the kitchen, Kelly was in the process of pouring the coffee into various multi-colored mugs which played with the shadows in the candlelight. Loomis stepped up out of the basement at just about the same time that Rachel entered via the livingroom.

Loomis asked Rachel, "Is your sister all right?''

"She's fine," Rachel answered.

"Good.''

Near the downstairs foyer, the doctor approached the deputy, and Logan turned.

"The sheriff has radioed for help," he said to the deputy. "They'll be here soon.''

Logan scratched his chin, the other hand remaining clenched to the riotgun. "Helluva night."

Instead of agreeing, Loomis replied, "It's not over yet, deputy."

The doctor buttoned his overcoat halfway, turned, and headed for the front door, knowing what he had to do; the task that at times he felt he was born to carry out. His hand reached out and grasped the deadbolt, turning the key and grabbing the knob to open the door. Logan jumped up to stop him.

"Where are you going?"

"The Caruther's house," the doctor said sternly. "That's where Jamie lives. That's where he'll wait for her. And that's where I'll be waiting for *him*."

"Leave Myers for the State boys," Logan insisted.

Loomis shot back a glance. "The State Police won't know what to look for. Or how to stop him."

"Do *you* know?"

Loomis could not answer that. All he knew was to exit out that front door; what he must do. The deputy reluctantly allowed him past, and Loomis pulled the door opened, disappearing into the night. The deputy watched as the figure in the overcoat strode quickly down the walkway, and he shook his head.

He closed the door and relocked it.

****

In the kitchen, Kelly was searching almost recklessly for a cup of sugar, accidentally knocking a tall glass from the sink and sending it crashing to the floor.

"Shit," she exclaimed, and, for the time being, she kicked a few of the shards over to a space on the floor near the plastic wastebasket.

As she did so, Rachel, who had been standing along the sidelines watching quietly, stepped close to one of the opened cupboards. She reached upwards and closed it, then pulled an object out from the back of the counter top. It was a sugar bowl.

"Looking for this?" she said.

Kelly turned to her and saw what the girl held, irritated. "Look, I didn't know you and Brady had anything going, okay?"

"You knew," she said calmly. "You just didn't care."

"He's not married or anything," Kelly said defensively. "I've got a right to do what's best for me."

This was one goddamn bitch, Rachel thought to herself. *She was a slut, there were no two ways about it, and the hell with the fact that she happened to be the sheriff's daughter.*

Rachel proclaimed dramatically, "Future home-wreckers of America, unite! Your future president has spoken."

Kelly appeared annoyed. *Not only was she a bitchy slut, but she was even a bitchy, conceited slut at that*, Rachel thought.

Kelly told her, "Wise up to what men want, Rachel. Or Brady won't be the last man you lose to another woman."

Rachel reached for a mug of coffee and splashed it across the girl's t-shirt. Startled, Kelly jumped back. The wetness didn't scorch her, and she was grateful to herself for making the coffee set in expectation for the lost sugar bowl.

"Have some coffee," Rachel said. She pushed past Kelly and descended into the basement and out of sight.

Unbelieving, Kelly stood there for a moment and absorbed the insult as her shirt absorbed the coffee. Angered, she stepped into the nearby laundry room and stripped out of the shirt. Her bra had been flung over to the other side of the couch when her father had pulled up in the driveway before; all her experience still didn't amount to an entirely successful last minute practiced dress. Pausing to wipe the slight wetness from her breasts which glistened in the moonlight streaming down from the nearby window, she threw the shirt into the empty machine and fished for one of her father's flannel button-downs. She found one, sorting through a nearby pile, slipped it on and buttoned it up.

For the life of her, she couldn't understand why someone like Brady would have the slightest interest in a girl as dull as Rachel. She threw it from her mind, not wanting to deal with such trivialities.

"Bitch," she muttered to herself.

****

Jamie was awake. Her eyes opened to the darkness of the bedroom, and she sat up and gazed around, her eyes accustomed to the lack of light but not being able to locate any sign of her foster sister.

Frightened, although not tremendously, at least not yet, she called out, "Rachel?"

But there was no answer.

Nobody's gonna get you while I'm around, Jamie recalled Rachel saying. *Promise.*

But Rachel wasn't there, was she?

Jamie cast her gaze on the semi-opened door.

Rachel will be back, she told herself.

But somehow there was a lingering doubt.

****

Rachel stepped over behind Meeker, and the sheriff acknowledged her presence with a weary smile. Then something else began to come in from the radio. As Rachel leaned over, Meeker lost whatever smile he had, his face turning hard and rigid. He listened to the radio cross talk among the stridency of squelch and interference.

". . . corner Elm and Gateway . . ." a voice spoke within the speaker of the black box. ". . . shot Ted Hollister by mistake. Musta been takin' a piss or . . ."

A new voice, deeper: "Is he dead?"

The other voice said, "Well, he sure ain't livin'."

"Aw, Christ," the sheriff muttered. He snatched up the microphone and spoke into it. "Is Earl Ford out there, this is Sheriff Meeker." There was now only static. *"Answer me, dammit!"*

177

More static.

Meeker angrily rose to his feet. Stooping, he grabbed his shotgun.

"Sheriff," Rachel asked, "what's going on out there?"

"Just wait here by the radio," Meeker instructed. "The State boys are going to send word once they're enroute. When that word comes, tell deputy Logan. You understand?"

Rachel nodded.

Meeker headed for the stairs, kicking his foot into a metal object as he went, nearly tripping, semi-exhausted.

Alone, Rachel was in charge of the radio. She was scared, not because she was by herself in a dark basement but, oddly enough, because of the pressure of responsibility. What the hell did *she* know about talking into a police radio? Hell, she didn't even know what *breaker breaker* meant. She thought she knew what ten-four meant.

God, what if she said the wrong thing? What could she do?

But in the midst of her panic, she realized that all she had to do was talk plain English. The God of the shortwave radios could punish her later. Or something like that.

She plunked down on the wooden chair in front of the small shortwave unit and stared at the instruments. The darkness surrounded her with the exception of the bright beam of the flashlight which rested on the bench beside the black, static filled box. She decided she would only touch it if some-one called for her.

Or if *she* had to call for someone.

Which wouldn't be necessary, of course.

She thought of Jamie upstairs. That girl didn't deserve this terror. What in God's name would allow something like this to happen to such a sweet little girl as she? It just didn't seem fair. But then again, the world didn't seem fair.

Nothing seemed fair anymore.

But there she sat, waiting impatiently for the State Police to come and rid the night of the darkness.

****

Out in the foyer, Sheriff Meeker turned the key which opened the deadbolt to the front door. Logan jumped to his feet from the easy chair and went to him. Before the sheriff stepped outside, he checked his shotgun momentarily.

Then, to the deputy, he said, "I'll be at Elm and Gateway. Doubt I'll be back before the troopers get here, but . . ."

"Maybe you ought to stay till they do."

Meeker said, "I've got a town full of beer-bellies running around the dark with shotguns. Who's next? Somebody's wife? Somebody's kid? I can't sit by for that. Not and carry a badge."

As Meeker proceeded to exit, Logan stopped him. "Watch yourself out there, Ben. Those beer-bellies aren't the only bad news on the streets."

"Just keep this door locked," the sheriff said, "and your eyes open."

Logan closed the front door once again and threw the lock in place, leaving the key in the mechanism. Sighing, he turned and proceeded back to the easy chair with his riotgun in hand.

Chapter Twenty-three

In the kitchen, Kelly readied the coffee for serving and set a steaming mug on a metal tray. Taking the tray with her, she walked towards the kitchen exit in the direction of the livingroom. The candle at the sink flickered with the soft breeze of her movements. On her way out, she banged her foot in the darkness of the space beside her, stubbing a bare toe against the leg of the kitchen table.

"Shit!"

She could feel the vibrations of the swirling of the coffee within the mug, but she could not detect whether or not it spilled.

She despised the darkness and cursed it, setting the tray down and massaging her throbbing toe. *Why the hell did there have to be a goddamn power outage this night, anyway?* She thought, *if there was a God out there, he was probably getting His kicks right now, watching and laughing as Kelly stood there, blindly aiding her naked, aching toe.*

This was great; just great.

Moderately flustered, she grabbed the tray from the table. With each new step, however, despite the pain, her frustrations began to dwindle. This coffee was for the deputy, and she wanted to be nice to him. God knew everyone was tired and at least somewhat spooked from this entire affair, and Logan was no exception. Besides, he was responsible for protecting them now. He was in charge.

And maybe, just *maybe*, she could get somewhere with him later. Remember, Daddy wasn't there no more.

Shadows played with her figure, and a shapely, black ghost fluttered and danced across the furniture and walls, moving as she did through the livingroom over the carpet and past the fireplace. The luminosity of candlelight accompanied her as she went, entering the foyer with tray in hand and setting it down on an antique lowboy. Kelly watched as Logan remained seated in the easy chair, head and back turned towards her, awaiting quietly for the slightest sounds of calamity.

Kelly spoke out, breaking the silence.

"Thought you might like some coffee," she said. Then, "Pretty boring out here."

Logan said nothing, remaining alert, ignoring her presence. She continued, "I wish they'd fix the power. So dark, I just stubbed my goddamn toe on the kitchen table. And at least we could have some MTV while we wait for the calvary."

Logan refused to reply. "You're coffee's gonna get cold."

Silence.

In the shadows, beside Kelly and on top of the antique lowboy, was an unlit candle and a book of matches which bore the words SOOKIE'S DEN embossed on the front. She grabbed the matchbook and struck a match, illuminating the terror-glazed pupils of Logan's mangled face, his body distortedly propped up against the foot of the lowboy in a bloody heap.

Kelly's hand went to her mouth, and she would have let out a horrified scream if it weren't for the sensation of her heart crawling up her windpipe to plop out of her widened mouth and into the stiffness of her palm. In a mixture of utter revulsion and shock, she stepped backwards as the figure of the one in the mask rose from the deputy's easy chair in full proportion, towering before her. Before she had time to think, the shape grabbed her; the immediate surge of agony swelled up from her abdomen, and it took but a split second's time before she realized she was impaled, the riotgun barrel already through her torso and the wood of the foyer closet behind her, and this terror was the last sensation she felt before she knew no more.

There was no sound, no struggle. The shape released her and stepped back, gazing in morbid admiration as the body of the teenage girl hung there before him, the wetness of her blood seeping from the obstruction protruding from her waist.

****

The radio began to chatter in front of Rachel's languishing eyes. She suddenly became alert, and her mind was filled with a sense of panic as she realized it was time to get on the ball.

Okay, this is it; don't worry about saying the right radio lingo, just go for it, babe.

From the black box before her, the voice was low and faint: "Should have cars dispatched in five minutes. Their ETA should be thirty minutes from that time. Over."

Rachel pressed the mike switch nervously. "Uh, okay, great. We'll be waiting. Uh . . . over and out."

Good. That was good, Rach. Maybe you'll grow up to be a truck driver. Pays pretty good.

She rose from the chair and headed for the basement stairs. Giving a slight yawn, she ascended into the kitchen.

The candle had burnt out near the stove, and Rachel had to feel her way around the table to make her way to the exit at the other end, past the laundry. Past the downstairs hallway, she made her way into the flickering glow of the livingroom, eyes casually searching for that retarded bitch called Kelly or for *anybody*, for that matter. There was a candle illuminating the front foyer where the deputy sat, and she moved in that direction.

As she stepped into the circle of light, she stopped short. It took a moment for the reality of it all to sink in, and when it did, it hit her with full, terrifying force. Eyes growing wide with shock and her mind coming alive with ultimate havoc, she managed to scream. As the cries took flight from her trembling lips, she backed away from the two bodies; upon a second glance she noticed that the deputy's head was pivoted completely around, the sightless eyes gazing past the impaled body of Kelly. The teenage daughter of Sheriff Meeker hung limply from the foyer closet door. Rachel looked down and realized she was stepping into blood-soaked carpet, each backwards step creating a slick splotching sound as if her tennis shoes were sucking into shallow mud.

In utter disbelief, her mind swirling as if in the midst of some morbid, drug-induced nightmare, she backed clear through the shadows of the livingroom completely until she backpeddled into the first few steps of the staircase. She found it difficult to breathe, the air coming in short, shallow gasps.

Her mind diverted to her foster sister, and she immediately cried out in anguish. *"Jamie!"*

She quickly scrambled up the staircase toward the darkened depths of the second floor, falling and attempting to relocate her footing, constantly spinning her head toward the nightmare over her shoulder and below. Finally, she made it to the upstairs hallway and rose completely to her feet. She ran, and when she arrived at the threshold of the master bedroom, threw the door open at once.

The bed was empty.

The room was empty.

Her eyes searched frantically. There was no Jamie. Her hand made for the light switch before she remembered there was no more light. A thought came across her mind: *there may never be light ever again*.

She stepped back in panic from the room's emptiness, turned, and headed once again for the staircase. Continuing to run, she descended into the candlelight of the downstairs livingroom.

"Oh God. Oh God," she panted, and for another moment lost hold of her sense of direction, her vision in a blur. She found her legs taking her down the hallway to her left—she thought it was her left—and as she turned the corner into one of the rooms she came upon the darkened figure. Hands shot out to her, grasping her shoulders painfully, and she let out yet another terrified scream.

It was Brady, shocked. *"What's going on?"*

Rachel couldn't catch her breath. Instead, her words came out in stutters and gasps, "Got to find Jamie."

"What we've got to do is get the hell outta here."

Rachel shrieked. *"NOT WITHOUT JAMIE!"*

"Look at those two back there," Brady yelled. "Do you really think Jamie stands a chance—"

"She's not dead."

Brady let go of her and ran from the hallway and out into the foyer, Rachel following after him mindlessly. He reached for the deadbolt, then his fingers stopped short as his eyes saw there wasn't a key. Something clinked across the section of the floor where the carpet ended, and he looked down. There, at his feet, was the end of the deadbolt key. A glance upwards revealed the other end stuck in the keyhole.

Brady panicked and turned to Rachel. "Is there another key? *Answer me!*"

"I don't know!" Rachel yelled back.

"Stand back."

Brady brought up his double barrel shotgun and fired into the deadbolt, shattering and blasting away the surface wood. The two stepped back as the splintered wood revealed a solid steel underlay.

"It's metal," Brady exclaimed, "goddamn *metal*!"

Rachel looked at it. "What's that mean?"

"It means we're trapped in this house."

Rachel turned suddenly and rushed toward the stairs. Brady followed her.

In the upstairs hallway, Rachel reached the top and cast her gaze toward the door to the master bedroom. Brady came up beside her and halted. As they both watched, the master bedroom door began to creak open, revealing nothing but shadows beyond. Upon pausing for a quick decision, Rachel took a tentative step forward.

"Jamie?" she called.

The door gaped open like a huge hollow mouth of a giant; its mystery beckoned her, and she hesitantly proceeded to oblige. At the opposite end of the hall, another door opened along the side, and amidst the sounds of a toilet flushing, out stepped the six-year-old Jamie.

Brady glanced her way, but there was little time to be relieved. At the master bedroom threshold, stood the motionless figure of the shape as if he simply materialized.

Jamie screamed.

"Get back," Brady shouted, motioning, "Rachel, get back!"

Rachel stumbled away as the towering shape began to advance upon them. Brady stood there, his shotgun up, aimed and ready. He pulled the trigger.

Nothing but dead clicks. He forgot to reload.

"Shit!"

The shape continued down the dark hallway rather quickly now, and Rachel scrambled over to her foster sister and grabbed her into her arms desperately. Just as desperately, Brady removed shells from his front jeans pocket and fumbled with them clumsily, hands shaking, until he finally broke down the shotgun.

Turning, he managed one final glance at Jamie as the little girl shouted, "Up Rachel. Go up!"

Rachel saw the attic stairs behind her and immediately began to climb them as fast as she could, her feet stumbling over empty space, her hands helping the little girl in front and above her.

Just as Brady managed the shotgun ready, the shape was upon him. It was too late. A shadowy hand reached out and fingers quickly grasped the muzzle as Brady fired into the side wall, creating a wooden crater to the thing's left. Without further pause, the shape heaved the teenager into the wall, a single powerful thrust, and Brady felt instant, sharp pains as ribs snapped inside him. He wailed. Using the shotgun stock as a club, the boy managed a furious swing through the air which cracked across the dark figure's temple, rocking the shape on his heels. Brady sprawled sideways, his world a fearful frenzy, whirling in every direction, his mind barely being able to issue a single thought.

"Son of a bitch!"

All he could do was swing the double barrel, using the might of both hands as he did so, blindly at first, hitting through the air and creating a short whistling sound. His thoughts began to form gradually once more, and he thought he managed another fortunate strike until he realized that the shape had caught the gun once again in its grip, and within the same moment it was out of his hands completely and flinging through the air; before he realized it, something—perhaps the gun itself or the shape's hardened fist, he couldn't tell what—drove into Brady's face, snapping his jaw and breaking teeth. The teenager reeled over and onto the hallway's carpet at the shape's feet.

With his remaining strength, Brady brought himself up along the side of the wall and staggered back upright. He brought a quivering hand to his face and felt the thick wetness of his own blood. Leaning forward and facing the shape, he stood there, frantic, wondering what the hell to do next. If he didn't do anything, he would surely die. If he did *something*, he would find himself dead anyway. But if he managed to do something *right*, if, by the grace of God, he managed to kill the thing, he would become the town hero.

Crazily, he snickered at the absurdity.

Nevertheless, he threw out a hard right towards the shape, connecting, the shape's head rolling to one side against the other wall. Brady was stunned at his own strength, and for one single final moment, he thought deliriously that he would win. He managed another right, his confidence building.

The shape lunged out suddenly and grabbed the boy's fist. Bones cracked and popped, and as the hallway became filled with Brady's cries of utter agony, he at once felt a tremendous hand grabbing hold of his skull, pressing, palms forcing to meet through intervening bone.

****

Inside the darkness of the attic, Rachel and Jamie were cowering within the far corner when they heard Brady's screams below; the screams stopped abruptly, punctuated by the wet crack of bone.

The older girl had managed to close the attic door, and upon hearing the sudden silence below, she rushed back feverishly and proceeded to throw chairs, end tables—anything she could find—against the door.

On the other side, the shape's hand grabbed the doorknob and forced the door open, foot by foot, until Rachel gave an urgent shriek and gave up, retreating back to the corner with her foster sister.

Cowering with Jamie, holding her close, she cried out to the figure, "Leave us alone! Please. Leave us alone!"

After an anguished moment, Rachel cast her gaze upon Brady's tool box. Letting go of Jamie, she anxiously rushed for it. She grabbed it, her mind and body overlooking the weight of the thing which, normally for a girl her size could have been quite heavy, and she threw it against one of the windows. The box smashed through boisterously, shards of glass flying onto the attic floor.

Outside, there was a narrow lip on which to stand, beyond that was a two-and-a-half story drop into the night. Carefully, Rachel leaned over and grabbed Jamie, pulling her up and onto her back. Desperately, the little girl held on, clenching.

Behind them, the shape loomed up the attic stairs, his dark figure rising slowly like the shadow of death itself, methodically and soundlessly.

Rachel whispered to Jamie before they set out to flee. *"Hang tight, Jamie."*

As quickly and as carefully as she could, Rachel stepped out the attic window and balanced on the ledge. She straightened herself, mindful of the tenuity of the wooden lip, gazing warily at the steep upward slope just inches away. She leaned away from the window and pressed her body against the cold slate roofing tiles, the brisk wind coming down upon her from one side bringing with it a bitter chill. Jamie weighed her down a bit, clinging to her back the way she was, gripping with her life, but Rachel forced herself to get used to it.

She couldn't fail. To fail meant to die, and for Jamie to die along with her.

As soon as she acquired a reasonable foothold, she glanced around her and caught sight of the chimney and the aerial. As swiftly and as steadily as she could, she proceeded to attempt a climb toward it.

When she was reasonably beyond the forefront of the broken window, she chanced a look back and in doing so nearly lost her handhold. Startled, she saw the voluminous effigy of her pursuer as he emerged from the shattered attic window and stepped over onto the roof. With mechanical precision, he made his advance toward the two girls, climbing, gaining.

Rachel continued climbing upwards and to the side, growing nearer and nearer toward the roof's peak. Jamie turned and gazed back down just as the shape reached a large, burly hand for Rachel's left ankle, then she quickly turned back to Rachel.

"Your left foot! Move your left foot . . ."

As soon as the hand came down, Rachel moved it away briskly, the hand clasping empty air.

Finally, at last, the girls reached the roof's peak. Rachel set Jamie down momentarily as she glanced frantically around.

There was nowhere to run. They were trapped.

And there, before them, was their murderer.

****

Halloween night had never been this cold. Perhaps it was merely the circumstance rather than the weather. Nevertheless, Rachel and Jamie were quite helpless there, on the very top of Sheriff Meeker's roof, and Jamie's uncle was there directly before them, ready to kill. There was absolutely nothing for them to do; no where to turn, nothing to fight with. Rachel lowered herself and scooped up her foster sister once again into her arms and held her close. She could feel Jamie shaking from the chill of fear, and she realized that a great deal of the shaking came from her own self also.

"Rachel?" Jamie called out in panic, "Rachel what are we going to do?"

The shape slowly advanced, towering over them in shadow.

Rachel tried to keep her foster sister calm, brushing her fingers gently through her hair nervously. "Try to go to sleep, sweetheart."

Jamie laid her head on Rachel's shoulder and shut her eyes. It was then that Rachel looked out into the darkness and spotted something.

A tree branch; it was over at the roof's farside, a bit more than a stretch away but close enough for a slim chance of escape. Quickly, just as the dark figure moved upon them mere steps away, Rachel hurried Jamie over to the branch and turned her over towards it.

"Jamie," she told her, "I want you to grab the branch. Grab the branch, and climb down that tree. I want you to hurry."

Jamie reached and strained, Rachel gripping her as close to the branch as she could. The shape was almost upon them. A few yards more, and . . .

Jamie's fingers brushed against leaves just shy of solid wood.

"I can't," the little girl cried out.

"Try!"

At last, Jamie found a firm hold on the branch and pulled away from Rachel, scrambling to the tree trunk. She looked back, screaming.

"Jump, Rachel!"

Just as the shape came upon her, she took to the air toward the tree. She managed somewhat of a hold, but it was the firm grip of the dark man behind her, yanking hard at her right ankle, which caused the fall. Breaking through a series of thin branches and leaves, she screamed until she thumped onto downward tiles of the lower roof and began to slide further. As she went, she reached out a hand and grabbed hold of the gutter. It held her weight for but a moment's time before it broke loose, sending the girl tumbling out of sight over the side.

There Jamie was, face to face with the very thing that wanted her dead, the two staring at each other from tree to rooftop: one staring in want and fascination, the other in fear and hatred.

The little girl climbed down the tree as fast as her six-year-old body allowed her to, her clown suit partially shredding and ripping against the bark and protruding branches. Halfway, she was forced to fight her way down among several branch groupings. Finally she broke free and tumbled downward to the grass lawn below. Springing to her feet, she ran around to the front of the house where Rachel's body had disappeared.

There she was; Rachel, lying quiet and motionless half in and half out of the hedges. Jamie rushed over to her.

"Come alive, Rachel." Kneeling, she wept and placed her foster sister's tilted head into her arms. She noticed a little dribble of dark blood running down the side of Rachel's head and neck. She sat there, rocking the teenager, trying but failing to bring her to her feet. "Oh please don't be dead, Rachel. Please, please don't be dead. Come alive, Rachel. COME ALIVE. OH, PLEASE COME ALIVE. *COME ALIVE!*"

But her friend and sister remained unmoving like a torn rag doll, eyes closed and mouth silent. Jamie continued to sit there with her, sobbing.

Behind her, a shadow rose. Turning, she beheld once again the shape, and she immediately scrambled to her feet. Leaving Rachel's body behind, she dashed across the lawn, nearly slipping on a streak of wetness, then reached the sidewalk and street.

The silent stalker continued in pursuit.

Down the street, at the center of the intersection, Jamie faltered minutely, considering a direction. Frantically, she chose one and continued to run in the street's all consuming darkness. Darting furiously, she kept her gaze before her this time, fearing that if she looked back she would see her nightmare man reaching out just inches from her back. In reality, the shadowy shape was in the distance, walking, seemingly taking its time as if in all confidence at winning its prey.

As she ran, she cried out, hoping someone in the town would oblige her, praying someone would be able to hide her and save her. "Help! Somebody, help me!!!"

As she went, doors began to open around her, but as soon as they opened, they closed just as quickly, and the sounds of locks and deadbolts echoed and rang through her ears and fed her terror and helplessness.

"Somebody please help me!"

There was no use. The nightmare man did not stop coming.

He would never stop.

Chapter Twenty-four

Jamie rounded the black street corner, silence encompassing her with the exception of her exhausted gasps for breath. She stopped momentarily, resting at the sidewalk, leaning against the shadowy outline of a birch tree.

She cast her gaze behind her, expecting her pursuer to be close at hand. As she looked, she saw no one. There was only the wind and the night. More concerned than ever, she shot glances all around her, expecting to see the shape elsewhere in an unexpected spot, stalking her from somewhere, ready to attack his victim. All was still silent.

As much as she could see through the night, the little girl saw nothing of the thing that chased her down the streets. She realized that she would much rather see him, knowing where he was, than suddenly stumble directly into his grip. She even glanced up into the thickness of the birch tree.

Nothing. Nothing anywhere.

But she hadn't contemplated that her stalker might possibly be around the bulk of the tree, and when she backed blindly into the figure, she screamed.

It was him.

No, wait.

The figure was much shorter. It knelt down, and Jamie found herself face to face with a wearisome and concerned Doctor Loomis.

"What are you doing out here alone?" he demanded.

At first, Jamie didn't know exactly what to say. Her mind was a whirlwind. But then the words *did* come, and she spoke them out, "Everybody's dead." Then, softly, "I just want to go home."

"No," Loomis said, "I've just come from there. That's the first place he'll look for you."

The doctor rose back to his feet and took the little girl's hand. He would have felt her nervous trembling if it weren't for the trembling his own hand generated itself.

"Come on," he continued. "We've got to get you out of here."

As fast as her legs could carry her, Loomis ran with the girl down the avenue, and within a few moments, unexpectedly, the power returned to the town. Porch lights, street lights—even the sounds of television sets, suddenly popped on. The streets of Haddonfield were illuminated once again. The two were somewhat relieved, but the strict meaning of the word was far from what they actually

198

felt. Loomis' mind was feverishly working on a location in which to hide. He knew, in reality, there was no such place. Reaching into the inside of his overcoat, he pulled out his 9mm pistol and held it firmly, expecting anything.

As they went, Jamie called out to him, "Is my uncle really the Boogeyman?"

"I'm sorry, Jamie," Loomis told her, "but your uncle is something far worse."

Chapter Twenty-five

A few lights came alive at Haddonfield Elementary School. During the night most of the lights were clicked off by the commands of a timer leaving on a few outside entrance lights. The school was illuminated just enough now as the city's power returned, driving away two young lovers from the bushes near the kindergarten classrooms. It wasn't merely the sudden appearance of light which spooked them into dressing as did Brady and Kelly, but the presence of people—what looked like an older man in a shadowy overcoat with a little girl at his hand. They made their way under the light; the two heading their way indeed turned out to be what they had guessed. The man and girl were actually hurrying, running, in the direction of the main entrance.

As Doctor Loomis and Jamie made their way across the sidewalk, passing a short chain link fence, toward the grade school building, they slowed, nearly exhausted. The night wind blew the swings on their chains in the playground beside them, the sound of shackles ringing through the darkness.

The main doors were chained and padlocked. Using his gun muzzle, Loomis broke the glass window on one of the doors, setting off a sonorous alarm. Jamie's hands went to her ears. She stepped back as the doctor aimed the gun at the chains and shot them apart. He pulled the doors open.

Loomis turned to the girl. "Come on."

Inside the school was sectioned by long hallways, complete with endless trails of lockers, glass display cases with various trophies, pictures and lopsided artwork, and neverending classroom doors. Frightening shadows and engulfing darkness accented the eerie scenery. The alarm continued its boisterous wailing.

"We'll hear sirens soon," Loomis said.

Jamie looked at him as they moved down the corridor. "Then we'll be safe?"

"Yes."

Jamie continued her gaze. "You don't believe that, do you?"

Loomis was silent for a moment. "You're very intuitive."

Together, they passed the main offices, a conference room, a janitor's closet; the hallway's shadowed corner was only a few feet away. Suddenly the shape of Michael Myers stepped out before them and lunged toward Loomis, grabbing him, hurling him through a nearby office glass door.

The deafening sound of shattering safety glass thundered above the wails of the grade school's alarm, raping the silent hallways. Panicked, Jamie turned and fled, shrieking, running down the hallway for escape. And at the dark figure's feet, Doctor Loomis settled into bloody unconsciousness.

There seemed to be no escape for the little girl. Her mind raced through her consciousness, telling her that this ordeal of being chased, being stalked relentlessly, was her destiny; a living nightmare that would never end. She fled down the maze of hallways and around corridors, missing the exit, thinking she may very well be safer within the confines of the school than out again on the streets. Perhaps she could find someplace really quiet to hide, some place deep within the grade school labyrinth. The hallways, blind corners and stairways seemed to be endless, as was her fleeing and her ability to flee. As she ran, the casual irrationality of her racing mind, that part of a person that steps out of the scene and watches as a sort of unbiased audience, applauded her performance at being able to endure the tremendous exhaustion which threatened to slow her down.

There, at the end of the next adjoining hallway, was an open classroom. Swiftly, Jamie ducked inside. She scurried past rows of desks toward the dark room's farthest corner. When she arrived at the outside corner of the room, she reached for the near window and attempted to force it open. It failed to give way; it was stuck. No. It was locked at the top, just beyond her reach.

Outside the room and down the hallway, the dark figure turned the corner and proceeded silently down the hall's length, closing the distance between himself and the opened classroom door.

Jamie skidded under the teacher's desk, pushing the chair aside and pulling it back as soon as she was situated underneath. It was a chance to catch her breath, however, she found she could not; she held it silently, in intervals, as she attempted to remain absolutely quiet and watched the door from the space between the floor and the desk itself.

Silence. No movement outside the opened door. There was only the constant darkness.

Fearfully, she waited. She couldn't dare make the slightest sound; the slightest sound, her own or otherwise, could bring the shape popping up from the shadows behind her or to her side, or she could feel the painful blade of a knife crashing down before her into her face.

She was waiting . . . waiting. . . .

There he was; the shape was entering the classroom. Jamie watched in terror as he made his way inside. To her shock he was crossing the room headed directly towards the teacher's front desk. The girl jumped in fright as his legs shoved desks violently from his path.

He knew where she was.

Jamie trembled uncontrollably as the shape drew nearer. Then there was the pounding—the thunderous pounding above her head. The shape was over the desk now, slamming fist and a knife into the surface of the top wood. It was like the sound of a sledge hammer, splintering, bashing the woodwork to dust.

Above Jamie's head, the desk began to crack, splitting open down the middle under the pounding force, raining woodchips. Desperately, Jamie slid from the space between the desk and the floor and jumped to her feet. She began to race, terrified and screaming, dodging the desks, disappearing out of the room, the shape missing her by a millimeter as her hair danced through his fingers as she ran away.

Down the hallway she went until suddenly an obstacle appeared before her. She slammed into it, the force causing her to stumble over onto her back. Turning, she saw through the darkness the subtle outline of a hall monitor's desk. A sharp pain stabbed at her right ankle and she grasped it, moaning both from distress and agony.

The shape reached the threshold of the classroom door. Seeing his towering figure, Jamie tried to stand. She could not manage to rise at first, and weight upon the injured leg sent her back down to the floor in pain. Half crawling, half hopping, she rose and leaned against the wall. However, her attempts at escape seemed futile. Behind her, the shape closed the distance between them with silent ease.

Just as she reached the hallway's corner; just when she thought, she *knew*, she would make it around and out of her pursuer's grasp, the figure grabbed her arm and turned her forcefully to face him.

There she was, face to face with the pasty white Halloween mask of death, his steady breathing a steady counterpoint to the relentless sound of the school alarm. She knew there was truly no escape. She knew she was finally about to die.

Jamie uttered one last scream as the blade from her executioner came down, slicing through the air.

Then there was steam. No; it was more than steam, it was the sudden freezing vapors of smoke which appeared between them. The shape released the girl and staggered backwards in confusion. Jamie turned.

It was Rachel. Thank God it was Rachel. She was holding a cannister of CO_2 directed at the shape's face.

"I knew you weren't dead," Jamie told her, both relieved and overjoyed.

Frantically, Rachel picked Jamie up into her arms and hurried down the corridor toward the nearest exit.

Exiting through the main doors, the alarm silenced within the last instant, the two girls met the brilliant beams of headlights sweeping around and before them.

Earl Ford's pickup swung up onto the sidewalk and stopped short of Rachel and Jamie, who nearly toppled over onto the pavement in exhaustion and relief, and lingering fear. Earl came up out of the driver's side, and at once the others jumped out from the rear bed, all men with rifles and shotguns ready to protect the good and blow away the bad.

"What's goin' on?" Earl called out to the girls. "We heard the alarm."

Rachel looked up at all of them, almost not believing her eyes—that out there, before her, there actually *was* help. She was near tears. "He's inside. . . ."

Orrin was taken. "Jesus, where?"

"In the school," Rachel directed.

"All right," Earl spoke out, determined, moving forward, "let's get this bastard."

"No."

Everyone halted at once.

"No," Jamie repeated herself. All eyes went to her, and immediately there was silence. "He'll kill you, too."

There was a certain matter-of-factness in the little girl's voice which stunned the men and cut through the air like a razor. Rachel gazed at the men in agreement, slowly nodding. The two were trembling, but their eyes were stern and serious; warning.

"We have to get out of Haddonfield," Rachel told them. "The State Police are on their way. Let them handle it."

A moment of silence passed between the girls and the men, then the thinnest of the bunch, Unger, spoke up first.

"I don't know about you, Earl, but that makes sense to me. Let's get the hell out."

Al said, "You saw the police station. Let the troopers have him. That's what they get paid for."

Earl stared at the grade school's dark expanse. There was no sign of movement anywhere within. Only silence and wind.

"Screw it," he said finally. "Let's get outta here. You two kids ride up front with me."

Everyone began to pile up into the pickup, some of the men gazing back into the dark mouth of the grade school's gaping entrance. Rachel and Jamie, however, did not. They merely did as they were told, gratefully and obediently, and climbed up into the front cab beside the hefty bartender.

The engine began to rev, and Earl swung back around to the street and accelerated off the sidewalk, burning rubber down the lane.

****

Inside the pickup, amidst the roughness of the bumps in the street as it made its way toward the outskirts of the town, Earl snatched up his C.B. microphone. As he did Rachel was reminded of the radio in the basement of Sheriff Meeker's place. She flinched at the memory of the nightmare she had left behind there.

"All patrols, all patrols," Earl said, speaking into the mike, "I got Rachel Caruthers and her sister in the truck. I'm takin' 'em outta town. Four-ten route. State Police are on the way."

"Packin' it in," came a deep voice from the radio speaker. "Good beer joint out four-ten. Maybe they got power."

The night passed outside the pickup as Rachel

held Jamie, gazing out into the blackness, remembering, knowing that for some ungodly reason the horror was not over yet.

Far from it.

Chapter Twenty-six

NOW LEAVING HADDONFIELD
COME AGAIN SOON

the road sign read. Earl's pickup was on the town's outskirts speeding along on route four-ten.

Rachel held Jamie tightly in her arms, rocking her softly, letting her know they were finally safe from the nightmare. As she thought to herself, Rachel realized how lucky they were, coming face to face with death as they did and escaping with their lives. She did little worrying as to what effect this sort of thing would have on Jamie for the remainder of her life; the little girl seemed to be, surprisingly enough, taking the whole matter like a real trooper. As for her own self—well, she'd rather not give it any thought. *Try not to think about how traumatic this all was,* she told herself. *Right now, let's just think about good things, nice things, and not about what just happened. Okay, Rach?*

Ahead, a convey of headlights rushed toward the pickup from out of the darkness on the other lane in the road. Sirens grew in volume as the State Police cars began to approach and race past on their way to the town which held the nightmare.

"There's the calvary," Earl declared, and at once he honked the pickup's horn to get their attention. At the same time, the men in the back bed began to wave their arms and shout, and Orrin took his shotgun and fired two shots into the air.

At the same time that Earl's pickup came to a halt at the side of the road, one of the trailing State Police vehicles did the same, turning. As soon as the two vehicles met, Earl proceeded to roll his window down and push his head out, calling to the trooper in the passenger side of the other car.

"Hey."

"You comin' out of Haddonfield?" the trooper yelled.

"Yeah," Earl told him, "Myers is in the elementary school. We're taking these kids to safety."

"There's a highway patrol substation four miles down the highway. You'll see turn-off signs. We've got officers on duty. They'll take care of you."

"Thanks."

Earl rolled up the window as the State Police car began to screech away to catch up with the convoy. In turn, Earl put his pickup in gear and accelerated down the dark highway.

As the vehicle moved further down the highway, it passed through wispy patches of fog. Soon, the vapors became curtains which the pickup sliced through as it continued onward towards its destination, visibility dropping . . . dropping.

Earl switched to low beams; the speedometer hovered at eighty. Earl was determined, yet his half of his mind was back in Haddonfield, thinking about how the State Police were arriving in front of the school; Michael Myers being driven out by tear gas or something, the firing squad ready, aiming . . .

Something jumped out through the fog in front of the pickup. Earl veered to the side, the wheels screeching, over into the dirt on the road's shoulder.

It was only a frightened doe. The animal bolted across the roadway into the blackness and the fog.

"Goddammit," Earl exclaimed, then gazed over at the two girls, momentarily terrified until they realized what had caused the commotion.

No one noticed the set of fingers closing over the tailgate in the rear, or the hint of white Halloween mask as it rose. The men who were sitting there, huddled in the rear bed, were too weary to look up. When they did, what their eyes beheld still didn't register within their brains until . . .

. . . it was too late.

Pulling himself up from the pickup's undercarriage, the figure of the very thing they thought they left behind rose to his terrifying fullness, towering above the exhausted men. It remained there, even as the truck began to move.

Orrin turned.

The others turned.

But their reflexes were too slow; the sudden

appearance was too unexpected. One by one, the shape grabbed them and flung them over the side like flimsy rag dolls. Orrin's shattered body rolled and settled limply into the thickness of the roadside weeds, eyes staring widened into nothing but darkness. Necks snapped, backs broke against asphalt.

The truck continued down the highway, the three in the front cab unaware of what had happened behind their backs. Casually, Earl glanced into his rear view mirror. His eyes registered an empty bed. His gaze quickly returned, and it locked on to the reality of what he was seeing.

No men. *What the hell?*

He turned to see for himself.

Suddenly, a hand smashed through the driver's side window, shocking Rachel and Jamie out of their half-sleep. Earl shrieked in unexpected horror, his hands losing control of the vehicle and his body losing control of his mind. The truck swerved violently. In one swift movement, the shape's hand gripped the bartender's neck and broke it, bone snapping, body twitching uncontrollably.

The girls screamed.

Rachel pushed aside Earl's body and grabbed for the steering wheel, shoving the corpse out the side door and then closing the door immediately. The shape's hand searched for a new victim. It searched for Rachel.

Rachel veered back and forth across the highway—swerving irratically, trying desperately to shake loose the figure of their attacker. A fist swung down hard against the windshield, smashing, creating a webwork of cracks. The shape's inverted masked face lowered before the girls, fully into view, the darkness where the eyes should be was hollow and vast.

Rachel slammed both feet onto the brake pedal. The pickup's wheels locked up instantly, screeching, throwing the dark figure from the truck's roof. The two terrified girls watched as he slammed down onto the surface of the road pavement before the truck and into the brightness of the headlight beams. It rolled thirty yards or so before it finally splayed out, face down.

Rachel gripped the steering wheel nervously, her mind racing within her head, her knuckles whitening. Beside her, Jamie cowered on the floor in front of the passenger seat, trembling, eyes wet with tears.

"Is it over yet?" she spoke out, her voice wavering. "Is my uncle dead?"

"I hope so," Rachel replied, half-whispering.

Then, through the windshield cracks, Rachel beheld the shape as it began to rise to its feet. Rachel shook her head in a fit of frenzy and disbelief, her face evolving, twisting with new anger. As the figure proceeded towards the front of the pickup, its movements zombie-like, Rachel threw the vehicle into gear and gunned the engine.

"No more!" she shouted out to the thing before her, and to all the powers of fate. *"NO MORE!"*

The truck raced directly toward the shape, speeding relentlessly, highbeams reflecting off the pasty white Halloween mask. The shape continued forward, making no attempt to avoid the collision.

The pickup slammed with full force into the shape, accompanied by a horribly loud and sickening sound, like a hand slamming palm-down onto the fullness of a tomato. The shape sailed backwards into the night, bouncing and rolling as Rachel made the truck come to an abrupt halt.

Rachel watched, Jamie continuing to cower beside her, eyes closed to the outside world.

The shape rose.

Rachel slammed down hard on the accelerator, the engine roaring once again. The pickup's rear wheels screamed on a cloud of blue smoke. Suddenly, the entire vehicle fishtailed, swerving, the rear end spinning forwards as the truck became a projectile, slamming into the shape once again, thunderously. The shape was sent flying backwards over the road shoulder onto a narrow dirt road, into the darkness and the fog.

The pickup raced after it, plummeting off a small, narrow embankment and onto the dirt road. The truck's highbeams found the shape once again coming to his feet. Rachel did not slow, but rather continued, slamming the truck hard into the shape's bulk, his body crashing violently with the truck's grill.

The shape came to his feet again.

Wham!

The body tumbled and crashed to the soil face down, unmoving.

Rachel panted like an animal, eyes wide, unblinking, expecting more. It was her will versus his, neither relenting until the very end when, finally, one must give up to fate.

The shape once more began to move, rocking to his knees slowly, rising up and moving again towards the truck within the beams of the head-lights, advancing one step at a time.

Rachel shifted into gear and planted her foot on the gas, burying the pedal into the floor, face full of cold determination.

"*Die*, you son of a bitch!"

The pickup rammed into its target head-on. The grill dented with the impact, penetrating the radia-tor. The hood broke loose from its mountings.

The shape wheeled backwards through the air, crashing hard, with enough force to break bones. This time, the dark figure did not rise. Spread eagled on his back, its fingers uncurled from the knife which he held.

Panting exhaustedly, Rachel rested her head against the sweaty steering wheel, weeping with both utter relief and misery, her nerves completely shot. She wondered what it was like to have a nervous breakdown, and she figured that if she wasn't having one then, she probably never would know. Jamie slowly got up from under the glove compartment. Sitting up, she stared out the shat-tered windshield onto the motionless configura-tion of her nightmare man.

The shape rested beyond the truck under a cloud of settling dust, the pickup's headlights just within his range. No sign of life. Nothing. Nothing but silence.

The sounds of engines announced two townie vehicles and State Police cars rushing down the embankment and the dirt road, slowing to a stop behind the pickup, bringing a darkened trail of dust along with them. Loomis climbed out of the lead patrol car, Sheriff Meeker along with him.

Truly relieved, Rachel climbed out of her own vehicle and walked over to meet the arriving convoy. At the same time, at first unnoticed by the others, Jamie climbed out and proceeded to walk towards the unmoving bulk of the shape. When she arrived, she slowly and reservedly knelt beside him. She saw that the body lay just shy of an abandoned well shaft which seemed to have been long since boarded over. She leaned over quietly, reaching for her uncle's bloody right hand, the hand which once held the knife, the hand which had viciously slain many victims. She held it with all the reserved quietude of a priest. Then very silently, she whispered something out to his stillness.

"I forgive you, Uncle Michael."

The milling crowded suddenly noticed where she was. Heads turned in urgent dismay.

Rachel's face filled with panic. "Jamie. Get away from him!"

There were other shouts, shouts from Loomis, from Meeker, telling her, warning her, to stay back or to not touch him—to get away.

But it was too late. Jamie turned just in time to

see the shape rising once again to his feet, Rachel screaming in the distance.

Suddenly, Meeker yelled to the little girl. "Jamie. *DROP!*"

At once, Jamie obeyed, dropping onto her belly. Meeker, the State Police, the townies, all opened fire upon the thing. Jamie covered her head and her ears as did Rachel who stood beside Doctor Loomis. The world came alive with a storm of bullets and double-ought, thundering through the night.

Michael was thrown backward, blown over the boarded well shaft. The planks gave way and the shape plummeted into the abyss.

Unger and another man came forward, dynamite sticks in hand. Each lighted one and hurled it into the shaft. Quiet. Then, suddenly, the shaft exploded, rocking the ground beneath their feet. The shaft began to collapse in on itself amidst a shower of debris and dust.

Gradually, everything began to fall into silence, highbeams cutting through the dust's whirling clouds. No one uttered a word; all eyes rested upon the space where the shape of Michael Myers had been, and they began to realize that, finally, he would never return.

Michael Myers was dead.

Chapter Twenty-seven

The nightmare was over. The Caruthers could try to live peacefully, knowing that time would ease the traumatic memories for both Rachel and Jamie. Darlene and Richard each took turns holding and hugging the two girls, exchanging and offering love where death had once stalked. Tears flowed amidst sounds of relief and joy.

A State Trooper helped a battered Loomis into the front hall of the home, over to Meeker, who shared in everyone's relief and sorrow, remembering his own daughter.

He turned to the doctor. "Is it over, Loomis?"

Loomis was too weak to smile. "Michael Myers is in Hell where he belongs. I hope we can forget about him now."

Meeker motioned to the family in the livingroom. "Those kids aren't likely to forget."

"They're strong," Loomis said. "They survived the ordeal. They'll survive its memory."

Rachel collapsed on the livingroom couch while Jamie wandered off towards the kitchen.

Darlene stood up and proceeded towards the stairs, speaking to her husband as she went. "I'm going to run a bath for Jamie. Talk to Rachel."

Richard got up and went over to his wife. They embraced. He watched her as she ascended the stairs. Richard turned and moved to where Rachel sat. Taking his daughter's hand, he sat beside her. They held each other, and Rachel suddenly began to weep.

Upstairs, Darlene ran the water in the bathtub. She gathered fresh soap and towels, humming something that sounded like *I'm Forever Blowing Bubbles*.

****

A mask was raised. Feet climbed the stairs to the second floor. The figure eased its way down the hall to where Darlene was, her back turned towards the door. A small pair of hands clutched a pair of scissors from the vanity. Darlene turned to her daughter, offering her a warm, maternal smile.

Her high pitched screams echoed throughout the upstairs rooms, finding their way downstairs to the startled souls in the livingroom and the front hallway.

Desperately, feet raced up the stairs. At the end of the hallway at the bathroom's threshold, all eyes beheld little Jamie, her hand clutching a pair of scissors, her body and hands stained with fresh blood.

And there, inside the bathroom, was the blood-drenched body of Darlene Caruthers, quivering until she finally dropped into a silent, horror-stricken gaze into nothingness. Forever staring.

Forever staring as was the little girl. Little Jamie, her eyes soulless . . .

. . . just like her uncle. Just like the evil. Pure evil.

Loomis stared in horror. Mindlessly, his hand reached for the pistol in his coat. Meeker and the troopers clutched at him, trying to stop him. The doctor's screams echoed into the night, outside, into the streets of Haddonfield.

For in Haddonfield, the horror never dies.